MICHAEL L. CLARK

Raven's
Lost Island

Library of Congress Control Number: 2025910052

Historic Traces Publishing
Pensacola, Florida

Hardback: ISBN 978-1-965756-09-6

Paperback: ISBN 978-1-965756-10-2

Ebook: ISBN 978-1-965756-11-9

Dedication

As an independent author who is self-published, putting together the right team to complete the project is challenging and necessary. The team that helped me with this project did an outstanding job.

First of all, I want to thank my family. My wife, Cindy, has stood by me and encouraged me throughout my journey as a writer. Her constant encouragement and her challenges have made me a much better writer.

My daughter, Casey Clark-Jackson, has been instrumental in providing advice about marketing and other aspects of the job. I couldn't have been as successful as an author without her help.

My daughter, Savannah Alexander, has been my go-to person when it comes to graphics. She has designed all of my book covers from the very beginning. I don't know what I would do without her.

I assembled a team of beta readers for the first time in my career. These eight individuals have encouraged me and made suggestions, especially post-manuscript. I look forward to working with them even more in the future.

They are:
Christie Schneider
Darlene Seaman
Jeff Neely
Julie Leffert
Marcia Wright
Shirley Smith
Sonja Loughton
Summer Brewer-Bryan

Thank you all so much for your dedication and willingness to help make this project the best possible.

Cast of Characters

Raven Ashworth - Born October 1, 1690, aka The Red Raven.

Pharaoh—formerly known as Batimkoo (Bah-tim'-koo)— is translated as My father's houses have many to feed. Pharaoh has been Raven's most trusted crew member and friend, who once served as captain of the *Matilda*.

Alexander—formerly known as Shujaa Shujaa (Shoo-dah' Shoo-dah') was captain of the *Nightingale* before the French sank it.

Attila—formerly known as Mtu Waoga (Mm-Voo-oh'-vuh)— is translated as a cowardly man. However, He was captain of the *Lady Falcon* and was anything but a coward.

Jeffrey Hamilton—quartermaster

John Ashworth—first mate and father of Raven.

Hadari (Hud-dar'-ee) —Translates: Danger. Hadari serves as second mate on *Raven's Destiny*.

Louis Hardy—cook

Jeremy Finch— junior officer. He would assist the first and second mates with duties on the ship's deck and take turns at the watch. Jeremy is also the ship's lead gunnery mate.

Isaac Finch —father of Jeremy and the ship's helmsman.

Andrew Greer — ship's doctor and carpenter.

Kujana wa Muziki (Koo-don'-nuh wuh Moo-zee'-kee)—Translates: Musical Youth. Muziki serves as the ship's signal drummer and crew member.

Mwanamke Simba (Mwah-nom'-kuh Sim'-buh)—Translates: The Lady Warrior. Simba is a warrior and special assistant to Raven.

Zachery Thacker —Ship's Boy who received a demotion due to his treachery.

Kifaru (Kif'-ah-roo)—Translates: Rhinoceros. Kifaru is another helmsman on *Raven's Destiny*.

Oscar Alejandro Rivera —A trade merchant on Port St. Felix and sometimes a partner to Raven.

Mtu Mdago (Mtoo-dah'-vo)—Translates: Little Man. Mdago is a crew member on *Destiny*, often found in the crow's nest.

Mwanamke Mtamu (Mwah-nom'-kay tah'-moo)—Translates: Sweet Woman - Mtamu was a female crew member on *Destiny* who spent much time in the crow's nest.

Mvuvi (Moo'-Vee)—Translates: Fisherman. Mvuvi was a crew member on *Destiny*.

Bila Meno (Bee'-lah May'-no)—Translates: Without Teeth. Bila Meno was a toothless, happy-go-lucky crew member on *Destiny*.

Seremala (Sail-a-mah'-luh)—Translates: Carpenter. Seremalao was a crew member on *Destiny* who often helped the ship's carpenter, Mr. Greer.

Shujaa wa Mfalme (Soo-dah' wahm foul'-mae)—Translates: the King's Hero. Raven rescued Mfalme along with hundreds of others sold into slavery, and he became the leader of the village that Raven set up at Port Gentil.

Jafaru (Dah-fa'-roo)—a member of *Destiny's* crew.

Juniper—a member of *Destiny's* crew.

Haggard—a member of *Destiny's* crew.

Rose—formerly known as **Ua Nyekundu** (Ooh-win'-ya-koon-doo). Rose was the wife of Pharaoh, who died on *Matilda*.

April—formerly known as **Mwanamke wa maisha mapya** (Mwhy-num'-kuh wah my-ish'-uh mop'-yuh), translates as woman of new life. She was the wife of Attila, who died on *Matilda*.

Melody—formerly known as **Wimbo wa usiku** (Wim'-bo wow ee-see'-koo)—was Alexander's wife, who died on the *Nightingale*.

Al Bagani (Al-bah'-von-ee)—King of the Mountain People.

Abobtu (Uh-bow'-tu) Son of Al Bagani.

Mshijana Mwimbaji (Mi-she-don'nuh Wim-bog'-ee) Daughter of Al Bagani.

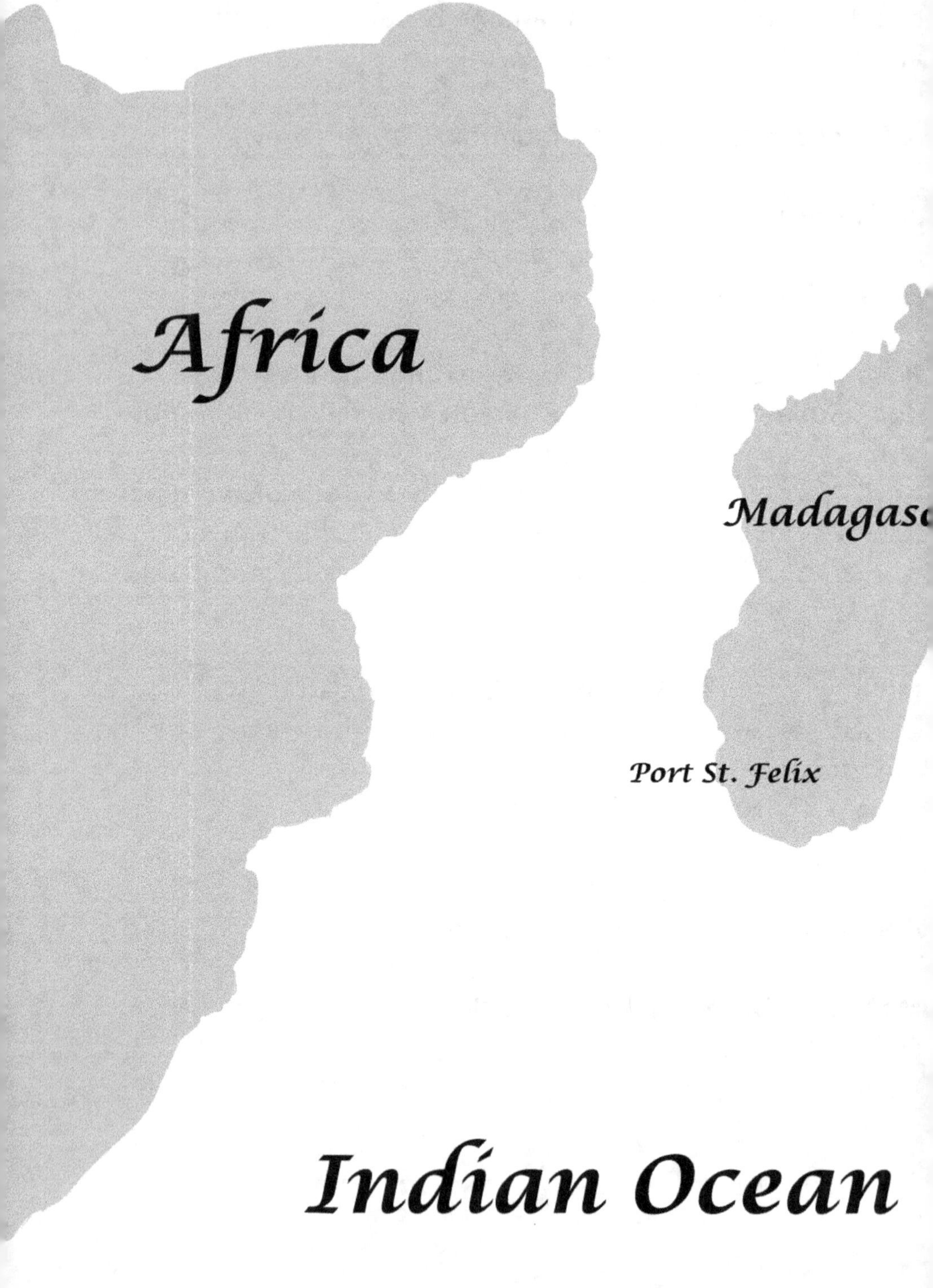

Africa
Madagasc
Port St. Felix
Indian Ocean

Chapter I

November 10, 1708

Cool November winds wafted across *Destiny's* starboard rail as she jounced through the waves of the Atlantic, sailing southward along the western coast of Africa, nearing the Cape of Good Hope. Temperatures were frigid for this time of the year, especially after crossing the equator. The 500-ton square-rigged ship carried her crew of buccaneers traveling to Port St. Felix on the southern tip of Madagascar. *Destiny* now supported fourteen new guns, seven on the port second deck and seven on the starboard, adding to the six guns she carried on the main deck: two on the starboard, two on the port, and one each at the bow and the stern. She still wasn't as armed as her captain would like, but it would do for now.

The ship's captain, Raven Ashworth, stood on the quarterdeck, her hair billowing away from her face as the wind gusted. Her long red curls danced in the breeze as she stood beside the helm. Now nineteen years old, Raven was most capable as a captain and well respected by her crew. Her juvenile monkey named Captain Billings rested on her shoulder as Raven watched her crew tend to the ship flying blood-red sails. The crimson sails told ships nearby that Raven was on the prowl. Merchant ships were aware of the notorious ship and its crew that sailed through the Atlantic in search of merchant ships carrying slaves from Africa to the new colonies of the Americas.

Raven noticed an unsecured rope lying on the ship's deck, so she called out to one of her men, "Mtu Mdago! Secure that line before someone stumbles over it."

"Aye, Raven!"

The young African male hurried to secure the rope, tying it to a belaying pin on the port rail. Most of Raven's crew were Africans. She had freed them from slave ships she had raided throughout the Gulf of Guinea. She had saved hundreds from a life of servitude and anguish, but lost many of them in a battle with the French Navy when three of her ships were sunk. Only *Raven's Destiny* remained.

France still had a price on her head. The bounty, now set at £1,500, kept Raven on the move. Any vessel she discovered in open water was either a threat or prey. Not even fellow pirates could be trusted as allies, especially in the Caribbean. Benjamin Hornigold, captain of the famous ship *Ranger*, had once been an ally but had now turned into an enemy. Raven's fleet of four ships had defeated Hornigold's fleet eight months earlier when Hornigold tried to capture Raven and the treasure she and her crew had collected from the depths of an island cave on the Cayman Islands. Raven's ships disabled the *Ranger* during their battle, leaving Benjamin and his crew limping back home to the Caribbean.

Not long after, Raven lost three of her ships in a battle with the French on the Cape of Good Hope as they sailed to St. Felix. Raven lost her three other ships, *Matilda*, *The Nightingale*, and *Lady Falcon*, along with more than half her crew and almost three-quarters of their found treasure. Her captains had been saved because they happened to be onboard *Destiny* during the battle, meeting with Raven as they made plans for the future when the French attacked.

Pharaoh, Alexander, and Attila now sailed with her on *Destiny* until other ships and crews could be captured to expand her army of pirates. A tall, well-built African, Pharaoh was the first one Raven had rescued from the clutches of slavery. They met when Raven was only twelve, serving disguised as a ship's boy on the original *Destiny*. She had befriended Pharaoh and bought his freedom. She would free four more, including Alexander and Attila, before *Destiny* was lost to the wrath of an Atlantic hurricane. They had been close friends and confidants ever since.

Raven watched the main deck as Jeremy Finch approached, inspecting the ship's rigging. Jeremy was only fifteen but was filling the position of first junior officer quite well. Raven smiled as she thought of how far the young man had come. When he arrived on her ship with his father, Isaac, Jeremy was only twelve and extremely timid. Raven took him under her wing and taught him to be a most capable officer. Jeremy's father stood at the helm, noticed Raven looking toward his son, and said, "You've been like a mother to him, Raven. I am indebted to you for that."

Raven smiled at Isaac and replied, "More like an older sister, Isaac. I'm too young to be a mother."

Isaac chuckled.

Hours after rounding the Cape, *Destiny* caught sight of Madagascar off the port bow. Mtu Mdago called down from the crow's nest atop the main mast.

"Raven, I see plumes of smoke coming from Port St. Felix."

Raven walked to the bow to get a closer look as she pulled out her spyglass. She spotted puffs of black smoke gliding through the sky. Next, she noticed columns of white smoke rising from near the pier at the port. She thought she could see two vessels mooring in the bay outside the port, but couldn't make out their colors. Someone was attacking St. Felix.

"Man the guns!" she cried out. "Mtu, as soon as you can, let me know who they are."

"Aye, Raven!"

Raven's crew scrambled to the cannons throughout the ship: one on the bow, one on the stern, and two on the starboard and port rails. The bow and stern guns were only four-pounders, but the rail guns were larger, eight-pound cannons. Fourteen new cannons were located on the mid-deck. Each of them was a sixteen-pound gun.

Raven told Isaac at the helm, "Come around wide, presenting our starboard guns, Isaac!"

"Aye, Raven!"

Pharaoh moved to the bow to join Raven as she anxiously watched the battle. He asked, "Can you see who it is?"

"No, can you?"

Pharaoh took out his spyglass to have a look. He scanned the coastline before them, searching for any indication of who was firing at the port city.

"Looks like a schooner or maybe a sloop. But I can't see the flag yet."

Raven turned back to Isaac and yelled, "When we come to within two miles, bring her 90º port so we can get a shot at them!"

"Aye, Raven!"

Destiny continued to sail, making a wide turn southeast from the Cape. Then, Isaac turned the wheel counterclockwise, making a turn north, bringing the ship within the two-mile distance Raven had requested.

As gunnery mate, Jeremy had his men load and ready the starboard cannons. Suddenly, a call came from the crow's nest.

"They're French vessels, Raven! Two sloops loaded with cannon!"

Raven looked through her spyglass again to see what the enemy ships were up to. She watched as both ships were intent on firing their guns at the city of St. Felix. She looked at the flag pole in the city and saw that Señor Rivera's signal flag was flying, indicating it was not safe for her to enter. Raven decided to take a chance that the French were not watching their backs because they were focused on their targets within the city.

Raven told Jeremy, "Since they have us outgunned, we'll have to make each shot count. Aim the starboard bow guns at the ship on the north side of the bay. Aim the starboard stern guns at the other. Try to hit their magazine rooms."

"Aye, Raven!"

Jeremy ordered his gunners to prepare each cannon for firing and wait for his signal. Once the cannons were loaded, Jeremy lined the sights for the proper elevation. He waited for *Destiny* to line up the shots as she moved through the waters.

"Fire!" he yelled.

The first cannon expelled its load, sending the eight-pound cannonball whistling through the air. Jeremy watched anxiously to see where the ball might strike the first ship. Without waiting to see if their aim was good, his crew fired the remaining cannons aimed at the first ship. Jeremy saw the first shot strike the ship on its port stern, sending shrapnel into the air. Men fell into the water and onto the deck of their ship from the concussion of the blast.

Without waiting for a response from the ship, Jeremy checked the elevation of his second main deck gun and ordered his men.

"Starboard stern gun, fire!"

Another shot rang out as the second cannonball whistled toward the target. Jeremy watched the projectile's arc as he returned to the first gun. His second shot struck the second ship, hitting her just below the waterline, causing the ship to begin to sink. Jeremy's crew had the mid-deck guns ready to fire. He rechecked his aim and ordered, "Fire!"

The slow-burning match was dipped into the fuse at the back of each cannon barrel and ignited the black powder again, sending more eight-pound projectiles through the air. However, by the time the shot was fired, the French vessel managed to get off a shot of her own, sending a 24-pound cannonball toward *Destiny*. Raven watched as the incoming shot sailed over their heads, missing her ship. Jeremy's shot hit the first ship on its port hull. The cannonball hit the magazine room where black powder was stored, which caused the entire ship to explode into a fiery blast.

Jeremy's first gun crew cheered at the sight of the first ship sinking into the sea. More cannon fire was sent from the second French vessel in *Destiny*'s direction. Raven called to Isaac, "Come about starboard quick as you please!"

Destiny altered her travel toward the French ship, avoiding being an easy target for the enemy, presenting itself as less of a target. The first two cannonballs landed harmlessly into the water on *Destiny's* starboard side, while another missed on the port. The fourth shot struck the bow of Raven's ship, but only just. Minor damage was done to the forward mast as the cannonball ripped through the foresail.

Isaac continued to steer the ship into a semicircle to present *Destiny's* port guns at the enemy. Jeremy and his crew moved to the port guns and began readying them to fire. Their target was closer now, with the ship having completed her turn. Jeremy took notice as he aimed his first gun at the remaining vessel. He adjusted the elevation for a closer shot and ordered, "Ready on the port bow gun. Fire!"

The first shot rang out, and everyone watched as the cannonball flew at its target and hit her again at the hull below the waterline. Men leaped from the ship into the water, trying to avoid being sucked down into the depths. The French vessel tried again to shoot its next gun, but it was too late. The ship sank, taking the guns and all hope with it.

As Raven's ship neared the port, her men stood at the rails, firing their muskets and pistols at the fleeing sailors trying to swim safely.

Two more French ships found themselves at the mercy of the Red Raven, but they discovered there would be no mercy.

Destiny pulled into port at the far south end of the pier, where she docked. The sails were lowered, and the bow and stern lines were secured to the dock.

Raven ordered, "Check the damage to the foresail and see if it can be repaired. Pharaoh, please check the foremast to see if it can be repaired."

"Aye, Raven."

Everyone set about checking the ship for damage, repairing, and finishing off any enemy still alive in the ocean. Gunshots could be heard whenever another Frenchman was found trying to swim to safety.

Raven walked down the gangplank as soon as it was secured to assess the damage to Port St. Felix. Many of the store buildings and tiny homes were destroyed. Others were consumed in flames. Women and children could be heard throughout the streets crying either from injury or fear. Raven mourned for them. The tiny city had become a second home to her. It had been a refuge for her and her men many times while being hunted by bounty hunters and the French Navy. Tears began to form in the corners of Raven's eyes as she meandered through the village.

Raven moved along the north road leading to Oscar Rivera's hacienda to see if her friend was safe from injury. As she made the right turn to reach Oscar's home, she was met by a familiar face—Rivera's most trusted man, Juan.

"Juan! Is Señor Rivera alright?"

"No, Señorita. He is not alright. The man from the boat hit him in the head many times. He does not wake up. He still breathes, but he does not wake up!"

CHAPTER 2

Raven rushed through the city with Juan as they made their way to Rivera's hacienda. When they entered the house, Raven found a young woman holding a tray with a bowl of water and towels, walking toward Rivera's bedroom. Raven followed her in to check on her friend, Oscar.

Raven sat on the edge of his bed and held his hand, speaking to him softly.

"Oscar? Oscar, it's Raven. Can you hear me?"

The young woman soaked the towel with water and began wiping the blood away from his face and the sides of his head. He winced in pain as she touched any open wounds. When Raven saw how severely her friend was injured, she asked Juan, "Could you send someone to my ship to get the doctor?"

"Si, Señorita. I will go."

Juan was not a young man, but he trotted down the road back to the docks to find Mr. Greer. Along the way, Juan witnessed many of the local people as they struggled to put out the fires that burned their homes and businesses. Children cried in their mothers' arms as many of the structures continued to burn, leaving many of the citizens homeless.

Once Juan reached the docks, and ran to *Destiny's* gangplank. He called out to whoever would listen.

"Hola! Hola!"

John Ashworth recognized Juan and walked to the gangplank.

"Buenos días, Juan. What can I do for you?"

"Señor Ashworth! The señorita Raven, she has asked that I come to get the doctor. Señor Rivera, he is in much bad shape. His head is hurt."

John looked around the ship and saw Zachery Thacker working on deck, swabbing the forecastle deck.

"Zachery! Go and fetch Mr. Greer. Tell him to bring his medical kit. Raven needs him to check Señor Rivera's wounds."

"Aye, Mr. Ashworth!"

Zachery leaped from the forecastle onto the main deck and entered the area of the ship where the officers' quarters were housed. He found Mr. Greer in the infirmary and relayed John's message to him. Andrew gathered up supplies he suspected he might need, put them in his medical kit, and followed Zachery out onto the main deck.

When Andrew approached John at the rail, John introduced him to Juan.

"Mr. Greer, this is Juan, Señor Rivera's aide. Raven has asked that you follow Juan to Señor Rivera's hacienda to check on him. He was injured during the attack by the French."

Andrew nodded to Juan and said, "Lead the way, Señor."

Andrew was almost as old as Juan but had no intention of jogging all the way to Rivera's home. However, they did walk quickly without overexerting themselves. Fifteen minutes later, they arrived at the hacienda and entered, finding Raven sitting at Oscar's bedside. Raven stood when she saw Andrew and said, "Looks like he was clubbed pretty severely. He will need some stitches."

Andrew asked, "Would you like me to stitch him up, or would you like to?"

Raven replied, "Oh, I'm out of practice. I'll let you take care of him."

Raven and Mr. Greer had worked together in the infirmary of the original Destiny for a few years. When Raven was disguised as a boy, she worked with Andrew, learning how to care for the sick and infirm. She learned much from Andrew about practicing medicine, but she had spent more time as a patient than as a physician over the past three years.

Andrew searched the injuries on Oscar's head, looking for indications that his skull may have been cracked. He gently pressed around the open wounds to feel if any movement occurred when he pressed.

"I don't feel any fractures. That's good."

He took out a straight razor and shaved the hair away from his wounds so that he could sew the wounds closed. He doused the wounds with a little alcohol, hoping to kill any infection, and sutured the wounds. When he had finished, Raven asked, "What do you think? Will he live?"

"I'm not sure. I think he should be alright, but he will need plenty of rest."

"Thanks, Mr. Greer."

Andrew turned to leave, but turned back and said to Raven, "I'm sure you could have taken care of him if you had the proper tools. I don't think you've forgotten how."

Ravens smiled and said, "Thanks again. I'm going to sit here a while longer. Tell Pharaoh he's in charge until I return."

"Aye, Raven."

As Raven sat next to Oscar while he slept, memories of sitting with her mother while she lay dying rushed back into her memory. *Was it seven? No, eight years ago*, she thought. Raven's papa was at sea working at the helm of a merchant ship while her mother grew increasingly sick each day. Eleven-year-old Raven scraped and scraped for every morsel of food she could find or steal. Her mother, too weak to get out of bed, was sentenced to bear the ills of consumption without the benefit of medicine or doctors.

Neither could be afforded. There was very little money. Papa had left them a little before leaving on his next voyage. However, rent on their little flat in Wapping was one shilling per week, and John's pay was less than £30 per year. So, money was stretched to the limits in order to survive within the confines of a large city like Bristol.

Young Raven often had to settle for rotten vegetables or moldy bread to feed her mother and herself. Vegetable broth was stretched sometimes to last weeks until the vegetables were disintegrating in the broth and invisible from both sight and taste.

Raven was stirred from her thoughts. Juanita, the young woman she had encountered when she arrived, brought in food and drink for Raven.

Juanita spoke Spanish as she set the tray of food in front of Raven. She smiled and nodded to Raven, then left the room. Raven hadn't realized that she was hungry. She moved the tray over to a table and sat down to enjoy her meal of black beans and tortillas.

After eating, Raven realized how sleepy she was. She looked around and saw a large leather winged-back chair in the next room. Raven dragged the chair into Oscar's bedroom and set it beside his bed. She sat in the chair, removed her boots, sat back, and rested her feet on the foot of the bed. Before she knew it, she had fallen asleep.

Something woke Raven as she reclined in the big leather chair. Startled, she jumped to her feet and searched the room, wondering where she was. She saw Oscar lying in bed, looking at her with amusement.

"Did you sleep well, Raven?"

"Oscar! You're awake!"

"Si, and so are you, finally. I have been watching you. Did you know that you snore?"

Raven allowed a slight nervous smile to his comment and changed the subject.

"How are you feeling?"

"Like someone hit me on the head with a club."

"Well, that's understandable since they did. Do you know why they clubbed you?"

"Something about my attitude and unwillingness to tell them where they could find you."

Raven replied, "I'm glad you are still alive. Is there anything I can get you?"

"A glass of wine would be nice."

"Before breakfast?"

"Ah, yes, perhaps with breakfast."

"I'll let Juanita know you're awake."

Raven walked out of the bedroom and into the kitchen to find Juanita. As she entered, Raven began to ask, "Juanita..." But Raven found Juanita being held by a man with a knife at her throat. The man was dressed in a French sailor's uniform. He was very young, maybe nineteen or twenty, skinny and terrified.

Raven asked, "Who are you, and what do you want?"

The young man was nervous and out of breath as he replied in French, "Ne t'approche ou je la tuerai!"

The only thing Raven recognized was, "Don't approach."

Raven tried to remember anything in French to calm the young man down.

"Pas de mal, pas de mal! Je suis un ami."

The man shook his head while continuing to hold Juanita. "Tu es le corbeau rouge. Tu vas me tuer!" Which translates to, *"You are the Red Raven! You will kill me!"*

Again, Raven only understood part of his response. Corbeau rouge, or Red Raven, meant he knew who she was. Raven heard movement from Oscar's bedroom and suspected he was trying to get out of bed to see what all the commotion was. She noticed the open window in the kitchen to the right of Juanita's assailant. Raven raised her open hands to indicate surrender as she said, "J'y vais. J'y vais." *"I go. I go."*

She backed out of the kitchen and retreated to Oscar's bedroom, where she found him trying to stand.

"Get back into bed, Oscar."

Oscar asked, "What is going on in there?"

"A man has Juanita at knifepoint. He appears to be one of the French sailors who was left behind. I'm going to sneak around back and get him through the window. Give me two minutes, then call Juanita to help you."

Raven pulled on her boots and sneaked out of the hacienda to move around to the back. She tiptoed near the edge of the outer wall until she found the open window to the kitchen. Raven raised her head to the edge of the window as she searched for the frightened sailor.

Oscar began his ruse. "Juanita! Juanita!"

The sailor held onto the young woman more tightly as he stared toward the kitchen door. Raven seized the opportunity as she drew her pistol, cocked, and fired at the young man's head in one motion. Juanita screamed when she heard the shot, and blood sprayed the side of her face.

The sailor let loose of Juanita and fell to the floor, dead. Raven ran back into the house to check on Juanita and Oscar. She ran through Rivera's bedroom and asked as she ran, "Are you alright?"

"Si! I am fine!"

As Raven entered the kitchen, she removed her other pistol from her belt and cocked it, ready to fire again if need be. There, she found Oscar leaning against the doorpost of the kitchen, staring at the young man lying on the floor with a bullet hole in his head. Juanita was curled up in a corner of the kitchen, sobbing beyond control. Raven stepped to Juanita and helped her to her feet, leading her into her bedroom in the back of the house where she could regain her composure. Raven helped her into her bed and covered her as Juanita continued to sob. She bathed the blood and brains from Juanita's head and face while the young woman continued to cry.

Once Raven was sure Juanita would be alright, she returned to the kitchen and began preparing breakfast for Oscar and herself. She cut up some mangos, sliced some bread, buttered it, and scrambled some eggs for them to share. As she started out of the kitchen into Oscar's bedroom, she remembered the wine he had requested. She went to the wine cabinet and selected a red wine to serve him.

As they ate their breakfast, Raven inquired about the attack on Port St. Felix by the French.

"Oscar, why did they attack your city?"

"What? I did not know this. I only know that they came here looking for you. They wanted me to tell them where to find you. When I told them I did not know, they began hitting me with a club. The next thing I knew, I was waking up with you by my side. What did they do to the city?"

"They set most of it on fire. When we arrived, we found many of the stores and houses were burning. The French were firing their cannons at your people, so we fired ours at them. We sank both of their ships and killed all of their men."

Oscar replied, "Oh, my poor people. What will we do now?"

"Don't worry, I'll find Juan and assess the damage together. You stay here and rest. I'll be back as soon as I can."

Chapter 3

When Raven arrived back at the little port town, she found familiar faces working to help the residents put out the fires of the burning structures. Her crew had left the ship to give aid to Rivera's people. Raven felt pride that her crew had pitched in to help the citizens of the tiny city.

Many of the residents of Port St. Felix were wandering about, not sure where to go because their homes and all their belongings were destroyed during the bombing by the French. Women and children wandered around the village in a daze, unaware of their surroundings.

Raven found Juan standing near the docks, speaking with her papa. She joined them and suggested, "Juan, we need to get these people some food. Is there anything left in the warehouses?"

"There is only one warehouse that was not bombed. It is in the back of the city. There is food in there."

"Wonderful! I'll have some of my men follow you there, and we'll set up a place to cook everyone a meal. I'll send Mr. Hardy along to organize the meal."

"Gracias, Señorita Raven. We will do as you say. How is Señor Riveras?"

"He is awake but still not well. We had a little mishap at his house this morning. A French sailor showed up and accosted Juanita."

"Oh no! Is she alright?"

"She is safe, and I sent her to her room to rest, so I need to return there and care for her and Oscar as they recover."

Juan asked, "What happened to the sailor?"

Raven realized the sailor's body was still in the kitchen. "Oh, I forgot. Papa, please have two men come with me to the hacienda to get rid of the body for me."

John sighed, "Another one, Raven?"

Raven shrugged as she replied, "I had to. He had a knife at Juanita's throat."

Mvuvi and Seremala followed Raven back to Rivera's hacienda. When they arrived, Raven showed them to the kitchen, where the dead sailor lay.

Mvuvi asked, "What should we do with him?"

"Whichever is easier for you: burn him or bury him. It makes no difference to me."

They scooped up the body and carried it out and down the street to the nearest building that was still burning. They swung the body back and forth a couple of times before letting it loose so it could fly into the burning building. Afterward, they walked back to the house to see if Raven needed them to help with anything else.

The two men entered the house and walked around searching for Raven. Seremala called out, "Raven?"

"I'm in here," she called from Rivera's bedroom.

Seremala stepped inside the bedroom and asked, "Is there anything else you need?"

"Yes, would you please ask Mr. Hamilton to join me?"

"Aye, Raven."

Mvuvi and Seremala left the house and returned to *Destiny* to find Jeffrey. They saw Jeffrey on the quarterdeck speaking with Jeremy as they stepped onto the ship. Seremala walked to the quarterdeck and approached the two officers without interrupting them.

After a moment, Jeffrey asked, "What is it, Seremala?"

"Excuse me, Mr. Hamilton, Raven asked that you join her at Señor Rivera's house."

"Thank you, Seremala."

Jeffrey left *Destiny* and began walking up to Rivera's hacienda. As he walked, he noticed many of the buildings were still smoldering from the fires the day before. Many of the residents were picking through the rubble, searching for anything salvageable.

When he reached Rivera's home, he knocked and waited. Juanita came to the door wearing fresh clothing but a haggard look.

Jeffrey asked, "Señorita Raven, por favor?"

Juanita replied, "Si. Entra."

Juanita led Jeffrey into Rivera's bedroom, where Raven sat and talked with Oscar. Jeffrey noticed that the window was covered to keep out the sunlight.

"Jeffrey, come in. Have a seat."

Jeffrey sat on a small chair near the foot of Oscar's bed.

Raven asked, "How are things progressing at the docks?"

"We're getting *Destiny* ready to sail again. Alexander and Attila found a tree suitable for making a new foremast. The old one received some damage during the battle. At first, we thought it was just the rigging and sails, but upon further inspection, we found that part of the old mast had splintered. We should be able to replace it with new rigging and sail in two days."

Raven replied, "That's fine. How about the people of Port St. Felix? Are we taking care of them?"

"Mr. Hardy and some of the crew have set up a commissary near one of the warehouses that wasn't damaged as badly. He's feeding everyone working on cleanup duty and the citizens of St. Felix."

"Good. Is there anything you need?"

"No, Raven. How about you? Is there anything I can do for you?"

"Thank you, no, Jeffrey. I will remain here with Oscar for the time being until he can get around on his own."

Jeffrey asked Rivera, "How are you feeling, Señor?"

"Not so good, mi amigo. My head is pounding like a hammer is hitting it. And the light hurts my eyes. For now, I must rest in the dark."

Jeffrey said, "Well, if that's all, Raven, I'll leave so Señor Rivera can get his rest. Would you like me to send Zachery here to help you?"

Raven replied, "Yes, why don't you do that? He can help Juanita with the work around here since she, too, has had a fright and is not feeling well. Thank you, Jeffrey. Please give my regards to Pharaoh. Tell him I will be back soon, but I have full confidence in him while I am away."

"Of course, Raven. Consider it done."

Jeffrey bowed to his captain and Rivera, then exited the bedroom and the house to return to *Destiny*.

Jeffrey was surprised by a call from the crow's nest the next day. Mtu Mdago called out, "Ship ahoy! Off the starboard bow!"

Standing on the quarterdeck, Pharaoh pulled out his spyglass to watch the approaching ship. Jeffrey approached the quarterdeck to join Pharaoh, John, and Isaac.

Jeffrey asked, "Can you tell who it is?"

Pharaoh replied, "It appears to be a merchant vessel. British, I think."

They watched the ship move toward the port. It was definitely a square-rigged ship flying a British flag. Pharaoh looked through his spyglass again and read the name on the ship's bow: *Roaming Myrtle*.

Myrtle was captained by one of her owners, Cyrus Pettigrew, son of the Earl of Pettigrew. Cyrus was younger than most merchant ship captains, only thirty-two. He had been sent to sea by his father at the early age of fourteen to wrangle away his rebellious ways. Finding a love for the sea, Cyrus chose to remain at sea after two years as a ship's boy and worked his way up until his father appointed him captain of his own ship, one of many owned by the Earl.

Roaming Myrtle pulled into the pier two slips away from *Destiny*, her bow facing north. As soon as she was tied to the docks, Juan approached the ship to greet the captain as he walked down the gangplank.

"Hola, Capitán Pettigrew. So nice to see you."

"Good day, Juan. My gracious, what has happened here?"

"The French, they have attacked us and burned our city. They bomb us with many bombs. Many people are killed, and many are hurt."

"Why would the French attack you?"

"I dunno! They did not told me. They beat Señor Rivera, too."

"Rivera? Is he alright?"

"Si, he is alive. But his head hurts much."

Looking around, Cyrus asked, "What happened to the French ship?"

"Oh, it was two ships. They are down there now." Juan pointed to the water below the pier.

"How did they get down there?"

"The Red Raven, she sink the ships. She save us all. She even help us clean up this mess."

Cyrus raised his eyebrows and said, "The Red Raven? Is she still here?"

"Si, this is her ship." Juan pointed at *Destiny*.

"Well, I've heard of the Red Raven but have never met her. Maybe I should go over and introduce myself."

"No, Señor. She not there. She is with Señor Rivera. She takes good care of him. She was once a doctor on a ship."

Cyrus replied, "Fascinating! Well, I have come to do business, but it looks like I may have wasted a trip."

"I dunno, Capitán. What are you wanting to sell?"

"I have rum, sugar, and textiles."

"Do you wants to sell or trade?"

"Well, since Señor Rivera is no longer in the slave business, I will need to sell rather than trade."

Jeffrey had made his way down the gangplank and moved closer to *Myrtle* when he heard Pettigrew and Juan's conversation.

"Pardon me, gentlemen. I couldn't help but overhear your conversation. Juan, will you introduce me to your friend?"

"Si, Señor Hamilton. This is Capitán Cyrus Pettigrew of the *Roaming Myrtle*. Capitán, Señor Hamilton is quartermaster of *Raven's Destiny*."

Jeffrey offered his hand and said, "How do you do, Captain?"

"Fine, Mr. Hamilton."

Jeffrey offered, "If you don't mind, sir, *Raven's Destiny* would be happy to purchase your goods if you are interested."

"No offense, Mr. Hamilton, but isn't your ship a pirate ship?"

"Well, on occasion, I guess. However, we are also a merchant vessel trading goods with certain tribes of people in Africa. We have a client who requires the exact contents you happened to be stowing in your cargo hold."

"I'm a little perplexed. Why wouldn't you just wait for me to leave this port and capture my ship rather than purchase my goods?"

"Oh, Captain, you have the wrong impression of our ship. Yes, we have overtaken ships and robbed them of their goods, but only those who are carrying slaves. You see, our captain has a soft spot in her heart for those who become unwilling servants to those who would oppress them. Since you are not holding slaves in your cargo, you have no need to worry. Uh, you don't have slaves in your hold, do you?"

"No, I don't."

"Well then, you have nothing to fear from us. We will make you a fair offer for your goods, and you may be on your way back to England."

"Alright, why don't you have a look at my cargo and make me an offer?"

Jeffrey replied, "Yes, I will have a look, but it will be up to our captain to make the offer and handle the negotiations."

Cyrus said, "That sounds fair enough. Juan, are you alright with this transaction?"

"Oh, I dunno?"

Jeffrey stepped back in, "Juan, don't worry. I'm sure Raven will be willing to pay Señor Rivera a finder's fee for what we purchase from Captain Pettigrew."

"Ok. Sounds good to me."

Jeffrey said, "Fine, shall we go and look at the merchandise?"

Cyrus called his first mate over to join them, "Mr. Watkins, would you take Mr. Hamilton below and let him inspect the merchandise? It seems we have a new buyer."

"Aye, Captain Pettigrew."

Watkins led Jeffrey to the lower deck to take an inventory of the merchandise he intended to purchase. Jeffrey inspected *Myrtle* as he walked across her deck. She was a well-maintained ship, clean and sound in every way. When they reached the lowermost deck, Watkins lit a lamp to show Jeffrey what was stored beneath. Jeffrey began by opening a sack of sugar to examine its contents and sample it. The sugar was brown, finely ground, and deliciously sweet. He sampled a sip of the rum from one of the barrels, which had already been tapped.

"Very nice, indeed, Mr. Watkins."

"Thank you, sir."

Jeffrey examined and counted the textiles of various colors and patterns—all high-quality cotton and wool fabrics. Jeffrey counted the bolts of fabric, the rum barrels, and the sugar sacks.

He asked Watkins, "Do you have a count of the goods I can compare my tally to?"

"Aye, we have two hundred barrels of rum, five hundred sacks of sugar, and one thousand bolts of fabric."

Jeffrey replied, "That is my count as well. I'll go and talk to our captain to see if we can come to an agreement."

Watkins led Jeffrey back out of the hold and onto the deck, where they once again met with Captain Pettigrew and Juan.

Cyrus asked, "Was everything to your liking, Mr. Hamilton?"

"Yes, Captain. Would you like to accompany me to Señor Rivera's hacienda to make the deal?"

"Quite so, I'm looking forward to meeting the Red Raven, whom I've heard so much about."

CHAPTER 4

As Jeffrey and Pettigrew left the *Roaming Myrtle*, Jeffrey glanced toward Pharaoh, who stood on the quarterdeck. Jeffrey nodded to Pharaoh, who raised his chin in acknowledgment.

A brisk bite of the wind blew across their faces as Jeffrey, Juan, and Captain Pettigrew walked through the once-prosperous city. The smell of burnt timber still lingered in the air. The citizens continued cleaning up the debris, burning much of it to make room for new construction.

As they walked, Pettigrew asked Jeffrey, "Tell me about your Red Raven. How old is she?"

"She just turned twenty."

"Really? So young yet so notorious. I presume she must be quite uncomely?"

Jeffrey smiled as he replied, "Oh yes, quite the hag. Toothless, with boils all over her face. She has a hump on her back and walks with a limp."

Juan snickered under his breath.

Pettigrew looked at Juan and realized Jeffrey must be having a joke at his expense. "You jest with me, Mr. Hamilton?"

Jeffrey smiled and replied, "Oh, quite so, Captain. When you see Raven, you will think she is the most beautiful woman you have ever seen. Even on her worst day."

"Oh my! Well, let us have a look, shall we?"

Jeffrey smiled and replied, "Oh yes, let's do."

When the three reached the hacienda, Juan led the way and escorted the two into the parlor to wait. He entered Oscar's bedroom to retrieve Raven. Raven entered the parlor expecting to meet Jeffrey alone, but saw a stranger standing with him.

"What is it, Jeffrey?"

"This is Captain Cyrus Pettigrew of the merchant ship *Roaming Myrtle*. He has come to sell his merchandise and was surprised to see that Port St. Felix no longer exists. I told him we might be willing to purchase his goods for our next voyage."

Raven replied, "How do you do, Captain?"

When Pettigrew saw how beautiful Raven was, his jaw dropped, and he stuttered as he said, " I'm w w well, thank you.

Raven asked Jeffrey, "Have you inspected his merchandise?"

"I have. He carries one thousand bolts of various cotton and wool fabrics, two hundred barrels of rum, and five hundred sacks of sugar. I counted each and every one."

Raven asked Cyrus, "What do you expect to receive for these goods?"

Pettigrew replied, "I was thinking about £2000."

Raven scoffed, "Did you get these goods from the king himself? What makes you think your load is worth £2000?"

"Well, I expected to trade for goods I could sell in Charles Town. I expected to receive that for my new cargo once we reach the Carolinas."

Raven sneered and replied, "You mean slaves."

"Well, yes."

Raven informed the captain, "Captain, haven't you heard that Señor Rivera no longer works in the slave trade? I'm afraid you've come to the wrong place."

Raven paused before offering, "I'll take your goods and give you £200."

Cyrus' eyes widened against the offer, "You jest!"

"Do you think so? Captain, let me tell you what would have happened had Señor Rivera still been in the slave business. You would have traded your goods for slaves, maybe 400. Then, you would have left here sailing toward Charles Town, where you would have encountered my ship. We would have overtaken you, robbed you of any gold or silver you might still carry, taken and freed your slaves, then tossed you and your crew overboard so that we might add your ship to my fleet."

Cyrus swallowed hard. Beads of sweat began running down his brow. He mustered his courage to reply, "You truly are a pirate."

Raven said, "Every day except Christmas."

Captain Pettigrew replied, "I think I'll take my goods somewhere else to trade. I'm sure you haven't shut down all the traders along the coast of Africa."

Raven looked at Jeffrey, who nodded to her. Then she looked back at Pettigrew and asked, "What goods?"

Confused, Cyrus half-shouted, "The sugar! Th th the rum! The fabric! What have we been talking about?"

Raven smiled as she replied, "Oh, that cargo. That's no longer yours to trade. We've already removed that from your ship."

"What!?"

"Yes. What once was yours is now mine. My men have already removed the cargo and placed it on *Destiny*."

Cyrus shouted, "This is outrageous!"

"Yes, isn't it?"

"Do you expect me to stand here and take this?"

Raven replied, "Captain, I made you a perfectly good offer of £200. Take it, or I'll take your ship as well."

Cyrus had never met such insolence. He rolled his eyes behind closed lids, took a deep breath, shook his head, and replied, "I'll take the £200."

"Good! Jeffrey will see to it."

Raven left the room without another word, leaving Jeffrey to escort Pettigrew back to his ship. Cyrus never said a word as they walked back to their respective ships. He muddled through his conversation with Raven again. He couldn't believe this young, beautiful woman had bested him in a transaction. He had always considered himself a good negotiator, but as he returned to his ship, he felt like a whipped dog with his tail between his legs.

Jeffrey said when they neared *Myrtle's* gangplank, "I'll be right back with your money."

Cyrus was still shocked as he replied, "Uh, yes, of course." Then, he waited at the gangplank. Soon after, Jeffrey returned and handed the captain £200 sterling silver.

Numbly, Cyrus said, "Thank you," then turned and walked up the gangplank.

Once he had boarded the ship, Watkins found him with a smile.

"Did you make a good deal, Captain?"

"Watkins, the only deal made was that we made it away with our lives and our ship."

"Beg your pardon, Captain?"

"We got a mere £200, and we get to keep our ship. We must steer clear of this lass, Mr. Watkins. She be cruel. Now, let's get underway before she changes her mind and takes *Myrtle* from us, too."

"Aye, Captain."

Two days later, Oscar felt well enough to get dressed and out of bed. He was concerned about his community and asked Raven to escort him so he could see how badly the city had been damaged.

As they walked through the streets, the people came out to meet their Señor Rivera. Some cried to him, while others spoke angrily about the tragedy that had become them. Rivera patiently listened to each person as they brought their troubles to him. Raven was impressed with how he dealt with each person, knowing each by name. She thought of her crew. Had she shown each of them the same concern throughout their time together? She didn't even know the names of many of those who had died in their battle against the French when Raven lost three of her ships. She was certain she knew the names of those who served on Raven's Destiny now, but for many, she knew little more than their name. Maybe, deep down, she thought it was easier that way. *If I don't know them, it wouldn't hurt so much when I lose them.*

However, if she knew more about each one, their likes and dislikes, the things they love, and the things they hate, she might be less likely to throw their lives away in some stupid battle. Raven made up her mind she would change that.

Raven and Oscar continued their walk through the once-flourishing city. Many of the people had already shown incredible resiliency by beginning new construction. Everyone worked together, cutting new timber, building new walls, and thatching new roofs. Raven did not doubt that the city would be rebuilt soon and would be even better than before.

After only an hour, Oscar was tired, so Raven walked him back to his hacienda and left him to rest in his room. As they entered the hacienda, Raven called to Juanita.

"Juanita?"

"Si, Señorita?"

"I'm going to leave now. I'll be back later to check on Señor Rivera. Do you need anything before I leave?"

"No, Señorita Raven. I take good care of Señor Rivera."

Raven smiled at the young woman, then turned and walked away.

As Raven returned to the ship, a light breeze blew from the bay, wafting her hair away from her face. She heard tropical birds singing to her as she walked alone. She realized as she walked that she rarely had the opportunity to walk alone. Someone in her crew always accompanied her. They seemed to always be on some mission. It felt nice to enjoy the sounds, smells, and warmth of nature around her. She allowed herself to smile. Smiling was something she rarely did anymore. Her life seemed so serious all the time. She was always needed by someone who needed her to make a decision. She would need to change that.

That night, Raven did change things. She had always dined alone except on rare occasions when one of her officers might join her as they planned some scheme. Tonight, she called Zachery to her quarters. When he entered, Raven said, "Zachery, would you tell Mr. Hardy that my officers will join me while I dine?"

"All the officers, Captain?"

"Yes, except for Mr. Finch. He will be in charge of the ship while we dine."

"Aye, Captain."

Raven collected several pieces of folded paper she had written on earlier that day and stepped out of her cabin and onto the deck. One by one, she met each of her officers. As she stepped up to the quarterdeck, she found John and Hadari standing next to Simba, who was learning to be a helmsman. Raven handed both John and Hadari one of the folded pieces of paper.

John asked, "What's this?"

Raven smiled and said, "This is your invitation."

"Invitation to what?"

Raven replied, "You'll see." Then she walked away.

John and Hadari each opened the folded paper and read its contents.

You are cordially invited to join the captain in her cabin for the evening meal. This will be a time of engagement between friends and family. No one is allowed to talk of business tonight. Please wear your best clothing as we dine together and make merry.

John looked at Hadari and shrugged. "I wonder what she's up to now?"

Hadari replied, "I don't know, but I don't think I like it."

Raven found Jeffrey standing with Pharaoh beside the starboard rail, checking the repairs made after their last battle with the two French ships in the harbor. After giving each man an invitation, Raven continued walking past them without commenting.

Pharaoh looked at Jeffrey and asked, "What is this?"

Jeffrey opened the invitation and read it. He smiled and said, "It seems we have been invited to a party."

Pharaoh asked, "What is a party?"

"Don't worry, my friend. It's just a time for friends to gather, relax, and have fun. It's much like one of your festivals but not as extravagant."

Pharaoh read his invitation, then remarked, "It says we should wear our best clothing. I suppose she expects us to bathe, too?"

"Yes, I guess you're right. We could all do with a good bath now, couldn't we?"

Raven walked to the forecastle and ducked inside the galley, where she found Mr. Hardy.

"Mr. Hardy, could you prepare a special feast for my officers tonight? We will be dining together in my cabin."

"What would the captain be wanting for her dinner?"

"I was thinking... roasted lamb."

Hardy grinned at Raven and replied, "That won't be a bit of trouble, Raven. How many will be dining with you?"

"There will be seven of us."

"Consider it done, Raven."

"Thank you, Mr. Hardy."

Raven left the galley and proceeded to find the rest of her guests. Along the way, she met Jeremy. He was standing at the ship's bow, inspecting the crew's work in scrubbing the outer hull.

"Jeremy?"

"Aye, Raven," he said as he turned to meet her.

"Jeremy, I will host all the senior officers in my cabin tonight for a get-together. I was hoping you would take over as duty officer while we dine. You will be in charge of the whole ship. Do you think you can handle that for me?"

"Aye, Raven. It will be my pleasure."

"Wonderful. I knew I could count on you. You've always been so dependable. You will make a fine senior officer someday, Jeremy."

"Thank you, Raven."

Raven looked around, searching for her last two officers. Attila and Alexander stood together on the docks, watching as the city was bustling and trying to reclaim their structures. Raven stepped up behind them and said, "Good afternoon, captains."

Together, they replied, *"Good afternoon, Raven."*

Raven handed each man an invitation and said, "Here are your invitations. I hope you can make it to my little dinner party. See you tonight." Then, she turned and walked away.

Attila looked at Alexander and asked, "What is a dinner party?"

"I do not know, but I hope there will be lots of rum there."

At 7:30 p.m., Jeremy, the watch officer, struck seven bells. Raven's guests began arriving at her cabin one at a time. Each man bowed to Raven as he entered and acknowledged her beautiful attire.

Raven owned one gown among her clothing. Her closet was full of seaman's garb: leather britches, linen shirts, leather jackets, and waistcoats. However, tonight, she was dressed in her jade-colored silk gown. Her hair was pulled up on top of her head in a bun, and her long boots were traded for a delicate pair of slippers.

The table had already been set, and the meal was waiting to be served as Raven had invited everyone to sit. She invited John to sit on her right and Pharaoh on her left. John bowed and accepted the place of honor with delight. Pharaoh had served with Raven the longest of all her men. He was the first she had saved from slavery, and he was her most trusted companion. The others took place around the table, with Jeffrey sitting at the far end, facing Raven. Jeffery's face showed how enamored he was to see her dressed in her finest attire. He was in love with his captain, even though she didn't always seem to return his favor. They occasionally exchanged loving touches and even kisses, but Raven had never said the words "I love you" to him.

All of her officers arrived wearing their best uniforms. Although they rarely wore the uniforms Raven had purchased for each of them when they were promoted, Raven delighted in seeing them wear the dress blues now.

As they sat down, Raven asked, "Papa, would you do the honor of carving the lamb for me?"

"I would be delighted, daughter."

John carved the roasted lamb and plated generous slices of the juicy red meat onto each officer's plate. Roasted carrots, potatoes, and turnips were passed around for each man to serve himself. Fresh-baked bread was passed around, and then Raven uncorked a bottle of wine and poured a glass for herself before passing it around to the others.

"I know most of you would prefer ale or rum, but I wanted to offer a toast with this wine first."

Each man held up his glass as Raven ceremoniously toasted their celebration.

"Here's to another year together as crew to our lady *Destiny*. May the year to come be our most successful as we serve together. Let no one think himself better than another, for we are all equal in God's eyes."

All replied, "*Here, here!*"

The next evening, Raven invited a new group of sailors to join her in her cabin for a party. Jeremy was the first to arrive, and he entered the very familiar confines of Raven's cabin. Jeremy had served Raven for three years as cabin boy before being promoted to junior officer. He spent much of his time in Raven's cabin looking after Captain Billingsly.

Others slowly filed into the cabin, beginning with Seramala. As he entered her cabin, Raven knew right away that Seramala had taken special steps to make himself presentable to her. She smelled a hint of lemons as he entered the room. Raven suspected that Seramala had washed himself in a pan of water and lemon juice.

"Come in, Seremala."

He shyly entered the cabin and sat at her table next to Jeremy, who had already seated himself. As soon as he was seated, two more men entered the cabin. Kifaru and Mvuvi walked in as they were welcomed by their captain. Then, Mtamu came next. Mtamu noticed how beautifully Raven was dressed. Being one of the few women on board the ship, Mtamu offered her compliments.

"Raven, you look quite elegant this evening."

"Why, thank you, Mtamu. You look lovely too. Where did you get your dress?"

"I bought it the last time we were in Mlima wa Dhahabu, visiting the mountain people. One of the women there traded with me for it."

Raven replied, "It's lovely and very colorful."

Finally, Bila Meno arrived to complete the party. As he entered the cabin, he smiled his toothless smile as Raven welcomed him.

"Bila Meno, thank you for coming. How are you?"

"I'm quite hungry," he said, smiling. "I hope we will have something soft to eat."

Raven smiled, "I had Mr. Hardy cook up some fish especially with you in mind."

"Nzuri! Nzuri!"

The party continued for the next three hours. Raven asked each of them about their lives before being captured by the slavers. She discovered that Kifaru and Mvuvi grew up together in the same village and were captured together while out hunting for game to feed their village.

Mtamu had a fascinating story to tell. Raven's crew had rescued her from the slave fortress at Lomé. Mtamu was there because the chief of her village had used her as a bargaining chip to keep his village from being attacked by the slavers. Twenty young women and thirty men were sent to the prison in exchange for the slavers staying away from their village. Many of the men were merely boys. However, some had been troublemakers, so the chief chose to get rid of them because he feared they might overthrow his command. Mtamu was one of the young women who had been trained to be a mwanamke mlinzi, or woman guard. They were trained to guard the women of the village, especially the chief's wives and children. As a member of the mwanamke mlinzi, Mtamu was forbidden to have any relationship with any man in the village. They were to be completely dedicated to the chief and his family.

Mtamu told Raven, "I was true to my oath as a mwanamke mlinzi, but a woman in the guard was jealous of my abilities. We often trained together, and I beat her in combat training one-on-one almost every time. She lied to the chief and told him I had slept with one of his guards. The chief sent both of us to Lomé to the prison. I found out later that the man who was also accused of breaking his oath of celibacy had been pursued by this treacherous woman, and he refused her advances. So, she set both of us up to receive the punishment of slavery."

Raven asked, "Is that man with us?"

"No. I think he left with some people from Port Gentil. I think maybe he went back to our village to get his revenge."

"You didn't want to get revenge?"

"No. I like what I am doing on this ship. I think I will do this for the rest of my life, maybe."

Each of the others shared their stories with Raven and enjoyed themselves as they dined with their captain. As they all left at the end of the evening, Raven smiled as she realized how much she and they had in common. She couldn't wait for the following evening to learn more about others in her crew.

Africa
Village of t
Mountain Pe
★
Five Points Cove
The Gulf of
Guinea

Chapter 5

Three days later, Raven's crew had finished the mast repairs and replaced all the rigging. Raven decided that the people of Port St. Felix were well on their way to rebuilding, so she said her goodbyes to Oscar, Juan, and Juanita and ordered her crew to get underway.

"Mr. Ashworth, please set a course for Mlima wa Dhahabu."

"Aye, Captain."

Destiny moved away from the port and began her cruise toward the Cape. Raven ordered the white sails unfurled as they began their trip to the Gulf of Guinea. Jeffrey stood at the ship's bow next to Raven as they began to pick up speed. The bow bounced through the waves in a slow, rhythmic pattern. Raven wore a long wool coat over her leather waistcoat to protect her from the chill that the Cape of Good Hope often presented. Her curly locks swirled around her face as Raven bounced through the waves. She took Jeffrey's right arm and wrapped it with both of hers, pulling him tightly to her side. Jeffrey looked down into her blue eyes and smiled. Raven nuzzled her cheek against Jeffrey's shoulder and closed her eyes. It felt good to be by his side. He felt warm and safe. She still wasn't sure if she felt love, but whatever it was, it felt right.

Jeffrey interrupted the quiet, saying, "Look."

Raven opened her eyes and searched for what Jeffrey was pointing out. A pod of dolphins swam off the ship's starboard bow. It wasn't easy to know how many there were because they constantly dipped under the water, but Jeffery thought there might be at least twenty. Then, one leaped from the water and dove back downward, disappearing for a while. Raven and Jeffrey watched together for several minutes until the pod changed course and swam away.

Jeffery interrupted their peace by asking, "How did your dinner go last night?"

"It went well."

"Who dined with you?"

"Mr. Greer, Isaac, and Mr. Hardy."

"Mr. Hardy? Who prepared the dinner?"

"Zachery Thacker prepared and served the meal."

"Really? How was it?"

"Zachery is an excellent cook. He may have found his calling."

"What did Hardy think of it?"

"Mr. Hardy tried very hard to find something wrong with the dinner. This needs more salt, or this was cooked too long. I think he may have felt threatened."

"Should he feel threatened?"

Raven asked, "What do you mean?"

"I mean, is there a chance you might replace him?"

"Absolutely not. No more than I would replace you as my quartermaster."

Jeffrey asked, "So, what brought about this sudden desire to hold these dinner parties? What do you expect to gain from them?"

Raven replied, "I witnessed something on St. Felix that I had never realized before. Did you know that Oscar knows every one of his people by name? He knows each of them intimately, as well as their children. I saw how they all revered him. They depended on him for their well-being. They knew they could depend on him for everything."

"Do you feel you don't have that same admiration from your crew?"

"Oh no, it's not that. I trust my crew; it's just that I don't really know them. Not all of them, anyway. I know them all by name, but I don't know them as people, and I want to. Do you know, most of the people we lost in that last battle, where *Matilda*, *Nightingale*, and *Falcon* were sunk, I didn't even know most of their names."

Jeffrey said, "Well, you can't really expect to know everyone on all your ships now, can you?"

"Why not? Oscar knows everyone in his city. There must be at least five hundred people there, and he knows every one of them. I think if I had known my crew better and knew more about them, I would be less likely to put them in danger."

Raven now began to cry.

"If I'm going to be responsible for the lives of so many people, I need to know whose lives I'm playing with. I won't make that mistake again. My crew shouldn't follow me blindly just because I freed them from slavery, and I shouldn't lead them blindly, not knowing who they are."

She sniffled and buried her face into Jeffrey's sleeve. Jeffrey changed position, moving his right arm to cradle her next to him as they stood on the bow. They remained there until Raven was able to compose herself.

Sixteen days later, *Destiny* crossed the equator into warmer temperatures as they entered the Gulf of Guinea. They continued northeasterly until they reached the seven-star-shaped cove that led to Mbini. They sailed into the center cove of the star to the shore of Lima wa Dhahabu or Gold Mountain. As they pulled close to the beach, they anchored far enough away that the tide wouldn't strand them aground.

Raven instructed Hadari, "Signal Abobtu that we are coming."

Hadari took out a conch shell he carried in a leather satchel he wore over his shoulder, then blew a signal to let the people of Gold Mountain know they were here.

Raven ordered, "Lower the dories."

Destiny now carried four dories, two on the port side and two on the starboard. Her crew lowered all four boats into the water and loaded them with the supplies they purchased from the *Roaming Myrtle*. Even with four dories, it would still take more than one trip to the shore to unload all the merchandise. Raven left with the first launch, taking twenty men with her. They unloaded the first delivery from the boats and set them on the beach while each unloaded boat returned to the ship to pick up more merchandise.

The twenty men left on the ship continued to bring up the rum, sugar, and cloth from below decks and load them into the returning dories. Unloading and delivering the goods to the beach took two hours. On the last trip, Raven's crew came over in the last boat, except ten men left behind to watch the ship with Jeremy and Alexander in charge.

Raven led the way down the trail to the mountain people's village with Captain Billings atop her shoulder. Barrels of rum followed her along the now well-traveled path. As she walked, Raven thought about how much the jungle had changed since her first visit almost three years ago. On their first visit to the mountain, Raven's men had to cut a trail as they searched for the mountain people. It took several hours for them to reach the place whose people now accepted them as friends.

Raven looked forward to seeing King Al Bagani and his son Abobtu again. It had been more than a year since she had seen them. She hoped they would have lots of gold to trade for the goods she now brought them. The textiles and sugar would be welcomed, but they would enjoy the rum most of all.

Abobtu appeared out of nowhere. He held a long spear in his hand and was followed by ten men who were blocking the path to the village. He held out his hand when Raven came within twelve feet of him.

Raven stopped and said, "Abobtu, how nice to see you again."

"Raven, you must go no further. There is sickness in the village. Even King Al Bagani is sick. The sickness is spreading to everyone in the village."

Raven asked, "What kind of sickness? Maybe I can help."

"Their skin is hot when you touch it. They sweat much, and they have bumps all over their body."

"Are the bumps red?"

"Yes."

Raven replied, "It sounds like measles. Some of your people may have come in contact with it while they were held captive in Lomé. I had measles as a child. I should be safe from getting it again. Let me come and help you. My men will leave the trade goods here for your men to collect. Then your men can carry it all back to your village."

Raven turned to John and said, "Papa, would you go back and ask Mr. Greer for as much laudanum as he can bring? If he doesn't have enough, tell him to send opium."

"Aye, Raven."

Raven followed Abobtu back to his village while John returned to the ship. The rest of Raven's crew stayed behind and waited for the gold to be returned so they could transport it to the ship.

When Raven arrived at the village, Al Bagani was the first person she visited. She found the chief lying on a mat in his hut, sweating profusely.

Raven asked Abobtu, "Can you bring me some fresh water and a towel?"

Abobtu nodded, then left the hut to gather what Raven had requested. Moments later, he returned. Raven began bathing the king with the cool water, trying to bring down his temperature. As she did, she instructed Abobtu, "Everyone who is sick needs to have this done to help bring down the fever. Can you send some of your people to do this?"

"Yes, Red Raven."

Abobtu delegated the task to several women who had not yet caught the sickness. Each of them scattered to various huts to administer Raven's request.

Two hours later, two of Abobtu's men arrived carrying a basket containing a bottle of laudanum and another larger bottle of a white powder labeled opium. Raven went from hut to hut with the laudanum, giving a dose to each person to help with their body aches. It wouldn't cure them, but they wouldn't feel as ill.

Once the laudanum was used up, Raven mixed another bottle by mixing the opium with honey and a little rum to liquify the powder, creating another form of laudanum. She continued giving each patient the medicine every six hours until they finally showed signs that the pain was dissipating.

Two days later, King Al Bagani was free from disease symptoms and returned to his regular duties as chief. Raven and Al Bagani sat together in the evening and shared a meal of roasted goat, breadfruit, and various other fruits. While they ate, they also sampled the rum Raven had delivered. Al

Bagani had become a massive fan of the intoxicating drink. It was much more tasty and satisfying than their own concoction made from fermented yams and honey.

The full moon rose high above Gold Mountain, illuminating the village. The skies were so clear it was as if every star that had ever shone was visible. Al Bagani had his servants bring out twenty-two small mahogany chests filled with Raven's signature gold coins, which his people had minted for her. Each coin contained enough gold to equal one guinea or one British pound and one shilling. There were roughly two hundred coins in each chest, so Raven walked away with approximately £4,400 in gold for goods she only paid £200 for. As long as the mountain people were willing to trade with her, Raven and her crew could do quite well in this endeavor. Of course, she had other ways of making gold for her and her crew, and freeing captured Africans from the clutches of slavery was still one of her primary endeavors.

Once her men loaded the last gold onto *Destiny*, Raven joined them, taking the last dory back to the ship. Once she climbed aboard, Raven walked up to the quarterdeck to give her instructions.

"Mr. Ashworth, please take us out to sea and set a course for Hispaniola."

"Hispaniola? May I ask what you have in mind?"

"I had a long conversation with Señor Rivera while he was confined to his bed. He, knowing how I feel about slavery, offered that many of his former merchant captains who purchased slaves from him didn't sail to the Americas. Instead, they traded with Spanish merchants bound for the west coast of Hispaniola. The settlement is one of the richest sugar exporters in the world, and they depend on slave labor to grow and process it."

John replied, "So we can free some slaves and get a load of sugar to sell at the same time?"

"That's the plan. We might be able to pick up another ship or two while we're at it."

John replied, "To Hispaniola, then."

John set a course heading west out of the Gulf of Guinea and turned northwest toward the Caribbean. Meanwhile, Raven entered her cabin for some much-needed rest. She walked to her bed and pulled off her boots while Captain Billings leaped from her shoulder to the head of Raven's bed. Raven finished undressing and climbed beneath her covers for what she hoped would be an uninterrupted night of sleep.

Puerto Rico

British
Virgin
Islands

Anguilla

St John's ◉

Montserrat

Guadeloupe

Dominica

Martinique

St Lucia

St Vincent
and the
Grenadines

Bar

Grenada

CHAPTER 6

Twenty days after leaving the seven-star cove, *Destiny* sailed into the Caribbean Sea. They sailed north of an island called Montserrat. Raven stood at the bow with Jeffrey as they sailed past and noted how much the island reminded her of the coast of Ireland with its green hills and valleys.

Jeffrey asked, "Do you know anything about this island?"

Raven replied, "Very little. I read what Christopher Columbus wrote about it. He's the one who named the island Montserrat, but there is little else written about it."

"How much farther to Hispaniola?"

"We have about three days until we reach the western peninsula."

As they stood together at the bow, Raven slipped her arm around Jeffrey's while they watched the waves dance across the ship's hull. The sea air was brisk as it whipped across Raven's face. She nuzzled against Jeffrey's shoulder. A flock of seagulls flew overhead, dancing together as they darted through the air. They squawked at one another as they circled in intertwining paths hidden in the sky. Raven enjoyed their songs and watching them dance together up above. She held onto Jeffrey's arm tightly and enjoyed the moment.

Fifty miles west of Montserrat, Seremala called from the crow's nest, "Ship ahoy! Twenty degrees starboard!"

Raven and Jeffrey looked to their right but saw nothing. Raven rushed to the quarterdeck and borrowed Hadari's spyglass. She searched the waters to the starboard of *Destiny's* bow. She scanned the horizon as she moved the glass from right to left, then back again. Finally, she caught sight of a vessel sailing away from them. The silhouette appeared to be that of a Spanish galleon slave ship. She was sailing west, which indicated she wasn't a treasure ship. If she were carrying treasure, she would be sailing east, back to Spain.

Raven looked back at Hadari and ordered, "Starboard, 20º. Full sheets."

Hadari called to the men, "Lower the blood sails! Full sheets! Kifaru, turn 20º starboard!"

Two men standing on the yardarm of the mainmast began switching out all the white sails for the crimson sails. The main sheet exhibited a black raven on its front. Men on the foremast and aft-mast released all the sails to gain speed. The race was set. They intended to overtake the Spanish vessel before it reached its destination.

Raven knew the galleon most likely supported more guns than she did, but she hoped to gain the element of surprise. If the Spanish ship were loaded with slaves, it would run deeper in the water because of the extra weight.

The waves splashed against *Destiny's* hull and over the rail as they sped through the sea. Raven called for Jeremy to join her on the quarterdeck. Raven's junior officer, Jeremy Finch, was in charge of the gunnery teams. It was a great responsibility for someone only fifteen years old, but he was very capable.

"Jeremy, ready all guns on the starboard side. At my signal, begin firing at the bow and working your way to the stern. Take out the rudder if you can. Try not to damage the hull. We want to disable her, not sink her."

"Aye, Raven."

Jeremy set one gun team to man the two cannons on the main deck on the starboard rail, giving them instructions about not sinking the ship. He went below to the second deck and set up three teams to man the starboard cannons below decks. The cannons Raven had installed on the second deck were more powerful than those on the main deck. She now supported sixteen-pounders.

Raven remained on the quarterdeck, lifting her spyglass toward the ship in anticipation of the battle that was afoot. Adrenaline began to flow through her veins. Her heart began to race. Battles at sea always excited the young captain. She enjoyed the thrill of outmaneuvering her opponents.

Raven's thoughts returned to her battle almost two years ago against the French fleet. Raven and her fleet of four ships went against the French while traveling to Port St. Felix to return Señor Rivera home after a successful treasure hunt. Raven lost three ships and more than a hundred good men and women in that battle. Now, she wondered if she might be making a mistake. Could they be successful against a Spanish slave ship with so much more artillery power than *Destiny* had? Her body began to convulse with doubt. Tears engulfed her eyes. She tried to wipe them away, but they continued to flow, blinding her. She continued to rub the tears away, but they wouldn't cease.

John noticed his daughter seemed to be struggling. He walked to her and whispered, "What is it?"

"Nothing, Papa. I've just got something in my eyes."

"I'm not so sure. Why are you shaking so?"

"Please, Papa, I'll be fine."

John stepped away but continued to watch his daughter. He suspected she wasn't well but had no idea how so.

Destiny began to gain on the Spanish galleon, but only slightly. The galleon captain adjusted by turning starboard to gain some distance between his ship and the one in pursuit.

Raven ordered the helmsman, "Hard to starboard! Let's see if we can cut him off."

Seremala turned the wheel to the right, making a 30º turn to intercept the galleon. Then, the galleon returned to port, trying to free herself from the pursuing ship.

"Hard to port, Seremala!" Raven ordered. She intended to match every move the Spaniard made, trying to gain distance on the galleon as she did.

Destiny pulled to within a quarter mile of the ship and was still gaining when a blast came from the galleon. **Boom!**

A cannonball arched through the sky, heading toward *Destiny,* but fell short by ten feet. The Spanish ship turned port again, trying to move away from the red-sailed ship pursuing her. Raven had the target she wanted now. She ordered Jeremy, "Ready the port guns! Take out their rudder!"

A call came back from the main deck, "Aye, Raven!"

Jeremy set up his port deck cannons to aim at the fleeing ship's rudder. He waited for the ship's rocking through the waves to line up with his shot. Just as Destiny turned to starboard, Jeremy called for the foremost cannon to fire. **Boom!**

The cannonball flew through the air, whistling through the wind below the clouds. The first shot was a miss to the right of the enemy's helm. The distance Jeremy calculated had been correct, but the alignment was off. He rushed to his second gun while his first gun crew reloaded the first cannon. Raven anxiously watched as her young officer lined up his next shot. Again, Jeremy waited for the rise of the ship through the waves of the sea to line up his shot at just the correct elevation and angle.

"Fire!" he ordered.

Boom! Another cannonball was released, and everyone watched as it flew toward the Spanish ship. Another missed shot as the cannonball disappeared into the ocean's depths behind the fleeing ship.

Raven moved to the helm and said to Seremala, "Give me the helm."

Seremala reluctantly surrendered the helm to his captain. Raven turned the wheel to the right and waited, feeling the wind change direction across her face. She watched the wind push against the ship's sails; she knew that distance was not their problem. Lining up the correct gun angle would be the most challenging part of this battle. The wind shifted, and Raven turned the wheel back to the left. She called out to Jeremy, "Get ready, Mr. Finch! We'll be coming back around starboard to give you your next shot."

Jeremy knew his shot would be approaching from the aft of the galleon, so he would have to wait to fire as the gun lined up with the rudder away from the ship's bulk. He had little fear of damaging the coveted vessel because a missed shot would fall harmlessly into the water without damaging the ship.

Raven watched her sails as she felt the wind change once again. She gently turned the wheel to starboard and watched as Jeremy's cannon lined up with the ship's rudder.

"Fire!" Jeremy yelled.

Boom!

Another shot rang out from the forward port cannon. Everyone watched as the projectile flew in a slight arc, lining up with the ship's rudder. They watched as a loud crack of breaking timbers could be heard. Wood splintered into the air and away from the galleon. Men screamed in Spanish and ran about the ship, looking to avoid any further cannonball fire. The ship's helmsman tried to turn starboard, then port, but to no avail. He had no control of the ship. The Spanish captain had no choice but to surrender. He ordered his men to raise their sails and wait for the approaching ship to give orders.

Raven returned the helm to Seremala. He returned to the wheel and asked her, "How did you do that?"

Raven replied, "It's all a feeling. You need to feel like you are one with the wind. Watch what she does, feel where she goes, then adjust to her will."

Seremala smiled and replied, "That makes no sense."

Raven turned as she chuckled and told Pharaoh, "Prepare a boarding party."

"Aye, Raven."

Then Raven told Jeremy, "Keep those cannons loaded and pointed at that ship. They may be feigning surrender."

"Aye, Raven."

Jeremy had his men ready the cannons on the main deck as well as the lower deck in case the Spanish sailors decided to fire against them. *Destiny* raised some of their sails to slow her momentum toward the ship. Raven kept watching through her spyglass as they drifted closer to the galleon. Pharaoh's boarding party stood at the port rail, brandishing their weapons and grappling hooks.

As they neared the ship, Raven called out to the captain in Spanish, "Have all your men assemble on the top deck with their hands raised. Prepare to be boarded."

The captain responded by turning to his men and ordering them to do as Raven said. Pharaoh's men threw their grapplers and pulled the two ships together. Once secured, they climbed over onto the galleon and held the Spaniards at gunpoint. Raven climbed over and walked over to the captain. The captain greeted her, saying, "I am Fernando Arguello, capitán of the Bruja Del Mar. What is it you want from us?"

Raven replied, "Bruja Del Mar, eh? The Sea Witch? I like that name. I think I'll keep it when I take over your ship."

"What do you mean, take over my ship?"

Raven replied, "We shall get to that later. Captain Arguello, you have cargo aboard?"

"Si, I have cargo."

"What is your cargo?"

"We are a slave ship. We have three hundred slaves onboard."

Raven remarked, "Really? I wager you started with more than that, didn't you?"

"Si, we started with more than four hundred. Pardon me, but who are you, and what business is it of yours?"

"Oh, how rude of me. I'm the Red Raven. When it comes to slave traders, I make it my business to punish those who would benefit from the misfortune of others. As you can see, most of my crew are African. They feel the same way I do about those who would enslave their people.

"Red Raven? I have heard of you. I did not realize you were so young and quite beautiful, I might add."

Raven noticed the captain. Although he was most likely twenty years her senior, he was quite handsome and very charming, not at all what she had expected to find on a Spanish slave ship. He was at least six feet tall and muscular, and his bronze skin seemed quite the contrast to his pearly white teeth. However, Raven wasn't sure yet if his charming manner was sincere or if he was setting a trap for her. She decided she should play coy with him.

"Captain, do you own this ship?"

"Ah, alas no, Señorita. I am but a lowly employee of the Spanish crown."

"Well, how attached are you to that crown?"

Arguello asked, "How do you mean?

"Are you willing to give your life for that crown?"

"Ah, I see. Well, now, what do you have in mind?"

Raven offered, "Well, you and your men have a choice to make. You can remain with your ship as part of my crew, or you can refuse and find yourself swimming back to Spain. However, if you decide to stay with me, beware. If I sense that you might betray me at any time, I will run you through with my cutlass and feed you to the sharks."

Arguello replied, "Well, Capitán, I can not speak for all my men, but I, for one, do not swim so good. I will accept your offer and remain on the *Sea Witch* to serve you as you wish."

Raven said, "You will serve me, Mr. Arguello, but not on this ship. You will come with me to *Destiny,* where I can keep an eye on you. My man, Pharaoh, here, is the new captain of the *Sea Witch.* Your former crew is now his."

Arguello was a little shocked to hear her statement. His ego was unwilling to relinquish his command of a ship he had become so fond of. But in the end, his life was more important.

"As you wish, Capitán. I will serve as you see fit."

"Good. Pharaoh, take control of the ship."

"Aye, Raven."

"Mr. Arguello, do any of your crew speak English?"

"My first mate speaks some English but not so good as your man, Pharaoh."

"Mr. Arguello, you may gather your personal belongings and bring them onboard *Destiny*."

"Si, Capitán."

Arguello excused himself and walked to his quarters to retrieve his personal items from his former cabin. He joined Raven back on the main deck for further instructions. Raven walked to the rail and asked Jeffrey, "Who do we have who speaks fluent Spanish?"

"I'm not sure. I'll ask around."

"Go, quickly."

Jeffrey left the rail and searched for a crew member who could fulfill Raven's needs. He found Jeremy and asked if he knew any of the crew who spoke Spanish. Jeremy replied, "Well, I know none of the Africans do. They can barely speak English."

He thought, then replied, "I think Mr. Thacker speaks Spanish."

"Zachery Thacker?"

"Aye. I noticed that he and Señor Juan sometimes speak when we are on St. Felix."

"Oh, Raven's going to love this."

Jeffrey looked around the ship, searching for young Mr. Thacker. He then spotted him coming from the galley holding a bucket of kitchen scraps to be fed to the pigs below deck.

Jeffrey called out, "Mr. Thacker!"

Zachery looked around to see who was calling. He noticed Jeffery looking at him and wondered what he had done wrong. Zachery saw Jeffrey beckoning to him, so he walked over to see what the matter was.

Jeffery said, "I understand you speak Spanish. Is this correct?"

"Aye, Mr. Hamilton."

"Where did you learn Spanish?"

"My family had a maid who was from Spain. She taught me Spanish."

"Your family had a maid?"

"Several, sir."

"Am I to understand you come from an affluent background?"

"I guess you could say that, Mr. Hamilton."

"How did you end up serving on a ship?"

"My father was one of the ship's owners. He wanted me to learn how the ship worked. He wanted someday that I would either captain one of his ships or manage the trade side of his business affairs."

"Does Raven know this?"

"No, sir. No one knows except you. My father said I should keep it to myself so the men didn't treat me differently."

Jeffrey said, "Come with me. Uh, leave your bucket. You won't be needing it."

Zachery set the bucket down near the rail and followed Jeffrey to where Raven waited.

"Raven, it seems Mr. Thacker here is fluent in Spanish. He has quite the background to which we have not been made privy to."

"Oh? Zachery, have you been holding out on me?"

"Aye, Captain. My father, who owned the Nightingale, told me not to tell the other men who I was because they might treat me as an outsider."

Raven replied, "Well, Zachery, you've done well since your demotion to ship's boy. You've worked hard without complaint. So, now I have a new job for you. You will serve here on the Sea Witch as a special aide to the captain. You will serve with Captain Pharaoh. Most of the crew doesn't speak English, so he will need you to translate for him."

Zachery's face lit up like a candle. Thank you, Captain! I won't let you down."

"Go and gather your things and come along then."

Zachery ran below decks to retrieve his few belongings and returned ready for duty.

Arguello returned with a trunk containing his belongings and prepared to move to *Destiny*.

"Just a moment, Mr. Arguello."

Raven stopped him before he handed over his trunk to someone awaiting on *Destiny*.

"Let's have a look in your trunk."

Nervously, Arguello said, "There is nothing here except my personal belongings."

Two men set the trunk on the deck and waited. Raven used the toe of her boot to kick open the latch and lifted the top with her toe once again. She told her men, "Search it."

Her men rummaged through the trunk, pulling out clothing, brass buttons, and grooming items. They found a smaller chest at the bottom of the trunk. One of the men presented the chest to Raven by holding it before her, allowing her to open it herself. The inside was filled with gold and silver coins—much too much for a captain's personal belongings. It was most likely money belonging to the ship for travel expenses.

Raven asked, "What have we here, Mr. Arguello?"

"That coinage is mine."

"I think not. It is much too much for a ship's captain to have. This is the ship's expense money."

Raven clicked her tongue, "Tsk, tsk, tsk. It didn't take long for you to show your true allegiance. Now, how can I trust you to serve on one of my ships?"

Arguello stared at the young captain and waited for what would come next.

"You have the heart of a pirate, but even pirates know you don't steal from your mates.

Chapter 7

Beads of sweat formed on the former captain's forehead as he waited for what would come. He nervously waited to see what Raven would say next. He inched his right hand behind his back and gripped a small knife hidden in the waistband of his trousers. Arguello raised the knife above his head and swung it downward toward Raven's chest.

Raven was waiting for him. She knew he would try something and had learned from previous mistakes. She blocked his hand with her left forearm, and the shock of sudden pain entered his belly. His mouth was agape as he tried to breathe. The Spanish sailors watched as their captain fell to the deck with blood pouring from his abdomen. The *Sea Witch's* crew gasped as they saw Arguello lying on the deck. Many began to step forward to aid him, but Raven looked at her crew and gave them a telling look to stop the Spaniards from approaching.

Raven then said to Zachery, "Translate for me."

Zachery stepped forward and stood next to Raven as she addressed the Spanish crew.

"Your captain, here, was about to steal from you and the owners of this ship."

She indicated the open chest of gold and silver on the ship's deck.

"I offered him the opportunity to join my crew and sail with me, yet he chose this. Now, you have a choice to make. Will you serve on my ship?

If you do, you will be treated fairly and receive your fair share of what we find, starting with the coins in this chest."

Raven pointed to Pharaoh and announced, "This will be your new captain. His name is Pharaoh, and he is a fair man. But, understand he will not abide insurrection. There will be no shirking, no stealing from your mates, and no cowardice. If you are ready to serve, come forward now and receive your first reward."

The men looked at one another, not knowing what they should do. One man, speaking broken English, stepped forward and replied, "I serve you."

Raven reached into the chest, selected two Spanish doubloons, and handed them to the brave sailor. He smiled and nodded to Raven, then stepped back.

Raven turned to Jeffrey and Zachery and said, "Get their names as they come forward."

Zachery met the man, asked his name, and gave it to Jeffrey to enter into the ship's log. One by one, the remaining men stepped forward and received their pay to remain onboard the *Sea Witch*. One by one, they turned to Zachery and gave their name. Fifty-eight men signed on with Raven's crew. Once they had all been paid, Raven moved to the next order of business.

"Pharaoh, let's see who we've got below decks."

"Aye, Raven!"

Pharaoh took Zachery and twenty of the new men below to free the enslaved people. They stepped down to the lowermost deck, and when they opened the hatch, the smell of death and decay was overwhelming.

Pharaoh told Zachery, "Get them below to unlock the shackles."

"Aye, Captain."

Zachery spoke to the men and led them down to the lower deck to free all those still alive. As they were freed, Pharaoh spoke to some of them and asked them to bring out their dead. Fernando Arguello had said there were three hundred slaves still alive at the bottom of his ship. He was forty-eight light in his count. More had died since his last count, and more were starving to the point of near death.

The dead were thrown overboard, while those who were struggling with their lives were laid out on the ship's deck and given water and food to help them recover. The remaining people were allowed to roam around the deck, and some were moved over to *Destiny* to allow for more room.

Jeffrey asked Raven, "What do you plan to do with them?"

"Just as we have always done. We will accept the most capable and willing into our crew and take the remaining back to Africa to make a new life for themselves."

"But where? Gentil?"

"Precisely. They should be able to make a nice enough life for themselves there."

Jeffrey suggested, "We probably need to resupply before we start for Port Gentil."

"Alright, we'll make a stop at Montserrat along the way. We should be able to resupply there. Let's get underway as soon as we can."

Captain Arguello's body was tossed into the sea with the rest of the dead; then, Raven moved back to *Destiny* to prepare for the trip back to Montserrat.

As they prepared to sail, Raven noticed a young African boy about thirteen years old wandering around the top deck. He seemed to be looking for something or someone. Raven walked over to him and asked him in Swahili, "Are you looking for someone?"

The boy replied with tears in his eyes, "My father. I have not seen him since we were put on the big boat. He was chained in another part of the boat from me."

Raven asked, "What is your name?"

"I am Keelie."

Raven recognized that his name translates as "Scream." "Did your father tell you why you were called Keelie?"

"Yes! He said, from the time I was born, I never ceased to cry very loudly.

"What about your mother? Where is she?"

"My mother died when I was born. I have never known her."

"What is your father's name?"

"His name is, Mlima Mkubua."

"Is he a large man, then?" Raven asked this because the name translates to "*Mighty Mountain*."

"Yes. He was the biggest man in our village. No one is as big or as strong as my father."

Raven replied, "Well, we shouldn't have any trouble finding him if he is still here, then. For now, let's get you something to eat."

Raven led Keelie to the galley and asked Mr. Hardy to fix the boy something to eat. Hardy rummaged around until he found two bananas and a mango, which he handed to the boy. "There you go, lad."

"Thank you, Mr. Hardy," Raven replied.

Raven took Keelie below decks and found him a place to rest. She set him up a hammock away from the crew where he could rest alone until his father could be found. Keelie lay in his hammock, which he found to be quite comfortable, while eating his fruit. Before long, he found that his eyelids were growing heavy, and he soon fell asleep.

Before the two ships parted ways, Raven returned to the starboard rail and called Pharaoh over.

"Pharaoh, I have a young boy named Keelie who is looking for his father. He hasn't seen him since they were put on the ship. Ask around to see if anyone knows of a man named Mlima Mkubua. Keelie indicated his father was a very large man."

"Alright, Raven. I will ask around. Is there anything else?"

"I'm sending Alexander over. He will still hold the rank of captain, but he will be your second."

"Aye, Raven. There will be no problems between us."

"Thank you, Pharaoh."

Pharaoh waved and returned to prepare the *Sea Witch* to launch away. Soon after they finished talking, Alexander moved to the *Sea Witch* to join Pharaoh. As they met, Pharaoh said to Alexander, "Welcome, my friend. I am happy to have you help me lead this crew."

"It is my pleasure. Where would you like me to bunk?"

Pharaoh replied, "I see no reason why we cannot share quarters since we share duties. We will seldom sleep at the same time, so we can alternate the use of the bed."

"That is fine with me," replied Alexander.

Unfortunately, Keelie's father wasn't located on either ship. Raven could only imagine the large man had perished while at sea, and his body thrown overboard.

The two ships turned back east and began sailing toward Montserrat. Two days later, they pulled into a bay on the island's north side called Little Bay. The occupants of Little Bay seemed much like the ones Raven had encountered at Treasure Beach on the island of Jamaica. Only these natives were friendly and seemed happy to see the two ships arrive in the bay.

The natives rowed out to the ships in long canoes. Both men and women welcomed the sailors into the cove as they waved and called out in their Arawakan language. The men on both *Destiny* and the *Sea Witch* noticed the women were not clothed above the waist. The Africans thought nothing of it, while the white men and the Spaniards all howled and whistled at the half-naked greeters.

Raven ordered four dories to be launched to resupply the ships. She selected sixteen African men to escort her to the shore. Many of the other men groaned when they realized they would not be allowed to go ashore.

Jeffrey asked Raven as she began to climb down into the dory, "Are you sure you don't want me to come along?"

Raven rolled her eyes at him and replied, "If you did, I'm afraid you would never get back on the ship."

Once they reached the shore, the natives led Raven into their village and offered her food and drink. She and her crew accepted their generous hospitality and sat down on the ground to share a meal of roasted boar, mango, breadfruit, and bananas. As they fed, Raven tried to communicate with some of the men by trying different language phrases. She tried Spanish, French, and English but was unsuccessful. Then, she heard someone who arrived at the party late—a white man who had lived among the natives. Raven stood to meet him and was pleased to hear him speaking English with an Irish dialect. He was a man of about forty years and walked with a slight limp in his left leg. He looked much older because his hair was snowy white, as was his long beard. His clothes were ragged and appeared to be the only set he might own.

"Sean O'Toole is the name, dear lady."

"I am Raven Ashworth, captain of *Raven's Destiny* and the *Sea Witch*."

Sean asked, "Captain, are ya? Well, I've never met a captain lass afore. How may I be of service to ya?"

"I need to resupply my ships before we sail for the Gulf of Guinea. We'll need enough food and fresh water for four hundred souls to last a month."

"My, that's a lot of supplies, eh? But, I thin we can supply you with enough to last your voyage. Tell ya what tho, we need ta hurry. We got ourselves a volcano in the middle of this island, and she's 'bout ta blow 'er top."

Raven asked, "Will the people be alright?"

"Shor dey will. S'long as dey stay near to da beach. Course, da food ya be needin' be in the middle of da jungle. So we's best git movin'.'"

Raven felt and heard a low rumble from far inland. She developed a nervous pang in the pit of her belly. She turned to her crew and said, "Let's get going. There's no time to waste."

Her men gathered their baskets and followed Raven and Sean into the jungle. About a mile from the beach, Sean showed them a mango grove surrounded by a forest of banana trees. They quickly gathered the fruits into their baskets, selecting unripe and ripe foods.

Raven asked, "Are there any orange or lemon trees about?"

"Aye, me, lady. Follow me."

Sean walked farther into the jungle and showed Raven a large grove of oranges. She and her crew filled more baskets with the citrus and began the trek back to the beach. They dumped their food into the boats, leaving enough room for two men to sit while they rowed back to the ships. Then, they made another trip back into the jungle for more.

When the natives saw what was happening, they gathered baskets and followed Raven into the jungle to help. Soon, they all had a relay of people delivering food and water to the beach while Raven's men rowed it out to the ships. They were supplied in less than six hours.

Sean and Raven stood on the beach waiting for the last dories to return to the island to retrieve Raven. Raven noticed the rumbling of the volcano seemed to be increasing. Looking toward the tall mountain in the middle of the island, she asked, "Are you sure you'll be alright? It looks like it's starting to flow."

"Aye, lass. She does it from time ta time."

"How can I pay these people for their kindness and generosity?"

"Oh, ya can't. Dey would be offended if you tried."

"Well, thank you, Sean. If I can ever do anything to help you, let me know."

"Well now, since ya mention it, would ya maybe be going back towards Ireland? I haven't been home in many a year. I've been stranded here since, oh, I dunno, five or six years."

Raven replied, "No, I'm sorry. We're not going anywhere near Ireland. We mostly stay around the coast of Africa and the Caribbean. Are you looking for a ride home?"

"Aye, I miss ma fam'ly."

"Why don't you come along with us? We can drop you off at one of the larger ports so you can catch a ride back to Ireland."

Sean's eyes began to tear up as she spoke to him. He sniffled and replied, "My lassie, dat would be such a bless'd thing. Are ya shor ya dun mind?"

"Sean, it would be my pleasure."

Raven and Sean stepped into the last dory and waved to the natives as they rowed back to the ship.

Gulf of Guinea
Simane
Port-Gentil
omboua
Ntchengue
Aranga
Mondorobé
Loanda
Odowwenga
Ozori

CHAPTER 8

Raven had one of her African crew escort Sean to the junior officers' quarters so he would have a place to bunk down. Sean noticed as they walked across the deck that hundreds of Africans were on the ship. Some were busy tending to the ship's duties, while others were meandering, doing nothing.

Sean was led into a room in the forecastle where he found four beds, one in each corner. The young man pointed to one of the beds and said, "You can take that one. Alexander was using it, but he is now on the *Sea Witch*."

Confused, Sean asked, "What be a sea witch?"

"The *Sea Witch* is the other ship. We just captured it a few days ago."

Sean asked, "What does ya mean, captured it?"

"The *Sea Witch* was a slave ship, hauling slaves to the Caribbean from Africa. That is what we do. We free men and women from the ships that are taking them away from their homes."

Sean was still puzzled, "Well now, what do ya do with all the people you free from the ships?"

"Some are allowed to join our crew, but most are taken back to Africa to start new lives."

"Who decided to start this venture of freeing slaves?"

"The Red Raven."

"Dat young lass who brung me aboard? She thought all this up?"

"Aye. She has been freeing Africans from slavery since she was twelve. I must go now. Raven will be wondering what happened to me."

Sean said, "Wait! What is your name?"

"Bila Meno."

"B b b what?"

"Bee-luh Mee-no. It means toothless." Bila Meno smiled, showing the one tooth still protruding from his bottom gum. Then, he turned and walked away.

Dumbfounded, Sean stared as Bila Meno hurried away. Then, he turned and looked at his bunk. He sat on the edge of the bed and noticed it wasn't uncomfortable. It was much more comfortable than the grass mat on which he had slept for the last several years. Sean decided to lie down for just a moment, but before he realized how tired he was, he fell asleep.

The ships weighed anchor and began sailing southeasterly back to the Gulf of Guinea. The wind was at their backs as they sailed past the numerous small islands that made a chain from South America up toward Puerto Rico. The skies were clear, and the sun shone brightly as they made their way from the Caribbean to the open waters of the Atlantic.

The *Sea Witch* sailed off the starboard stern of *Destiny* as they traveled through the dark blue waters leading to Port Gentil. Once again, Raven stood on the ship's bow, feeling the wind blow through her hair. Captain Billings sat atop her shoulder, squeaking at the pelicans flying in a V-formation along the ship's starboard rail. Raven munched on a banana while also feeding the monkey small pieces.

Jeffrey walked up and stood next to her. The two remained silent for a while. Captain Billings reached over and grabbed Jeffrey's ear. Jeffrey pulled away and wiped the sticky banana residue from his ear.

"What are you thinking about, Raven?"

"Nothing, and everything. Jeffrey, what would you be doing if you could do or be anything in the world?"

"Oh, I don't know. As long as I'm with you, I don't care what I do."

Raven curiously glared at Jeffrey as she replied, "Really? You have no ambition of your own?"

Jeffrey glanced around to see who might be close by, listening. "Raven, it wouldn't matter to me if I were a prisoner living in a dungeon, stranded on a deserted island, or in a rich palace. As long as I could be with you, nothing else matters."

"Really? Jeffrey, why would you say such a thing?"

Jeffrey grinned as he responded, "Don't you know, Raven? Haven't you figured it out yet? Raven, I'm in love with you. I fell in love with you the moment we met."

"But what if I don't want you to love me?"

"Raven, you may be my captain, but you can not control who I love or don't love. Only my heart can have a say in that matter."

Although Raven was shocked that Jeffrey had spoken the words aloud, she had never decided on the matter in her own mind.

"But, what if I don't decide to love you back?"

Jeffrey replied, "It matters not to me. I will still love you. It would be a struggle. It would be uncomfortable for me to be around you, knowing you don't have the same feelings for me that I have for you. But, in the end, I would still love you. I will always love you."

Raven paused before saying, "I suppose you want me to say it back to you."

"Not if you don't mean it."

"To be honest, Jeffrey, I don't know if I love you or not. I have feelings for you; I like being near you. But love? I'm not sure about love."

Jeffrey replied, "It's alright. I'm in no hurry. I will not push you on the matter. Just allow me to be near you, is all I ask."

Raven nodded to him and turned her attention back to the horizon. Her mind searched the distance of the sea for answers she could not find. Jeffrey squeezed her left shoulder, turned, and walked away.

Three weeks later, *Raven's Destiny* and the *Sea Witch* pulled into Port Gentil in the Gulf of Guinea. Shujaa wa Mfalme and two other men were on the shore fishing when Raven arrived. The Spaniards onboard the *Sea Witch* and the newly freed Africans witnessed the skeletal remains of men hanging from the trees along the beach. Many of the Spaniards crossed themselves and began reciting prayers under their breath as they saw the dead hanging among the trees.

Miguel Ramirez, the Spaniard serving as Pharaoh's first mate, turned to Pharaoh and asked, "What is this blasphemy? Why have you brought us here?"

Surprised that Ramirez spoke English, Pharaoh replied, "This is not blasphemy. This is a warning. The Red Raven hanged these men as a warning to those who would partake in the capture and selling of slaves. You and the others were lucky that you agreed to come along as crew. Had you not, you, too, could be hanging from a tree on some other island or worse."

Miguel inquired, "The Raven has truly done this?"

"Aye, and much worse. She looks upon those who would enslave others with complete disdain."

"How long has she been freeing the slaves?"

Pharaoh replied, "I was the first she freed. She was only twelve years old and was disguised as a boy working on a merchant ship. She befriended me and taught me to speak English and how to be a sailor. When we reached our destination, Charles Town, she implored her captain to allow her to buy my freedom, which he granted after much persuasion on her part. A year later, she added two more, and another year later, an additional two. We have faithfully served her ever since."

Miguel asked, "What is this place? Why do the dead hang from the trees?"

"A man named Andre Noel Arsenault once operated an arms factory here. He also ran a slave market here. Raven allowed him to continue his arms factory if he would no longer deal in slavery. He chose to ignore her. When she found out he was still selling slaves, she came back and destroyed the village and hanged everyone. Their bodies were left in the trees as a warning to all who would be involved in slave trading."

Miguel asked, "Señor Pharaoh, why does she do this? Could she not make more money as a merchant capitán?"

"It isn't about making money. We make money, but that isn't why we do it. I do not know why, but Raven is sympathetic to the downtrod-den—those who can't help themselves. Maybe something happened to her as a child that made her this way. But those of us who she has freed will follow her to the death, and some of us have."

Raven called out to Pharaoh, "Pharaoh, let's get these people unloaded and see what we have!"

"Aye, Raven!"

Pharaoh had his Spaniards unload the Africans from the *Sea Witch* while Raven's men unloaded them from *Destiny*. Nearly three hundred of them stood on the beach at Port Gentil when Shujaa wa Mfalme walked over to see what was happening.

Raven greeted him as he approached, "Salamu, Mfalme."

"Salamu, Red Raven. What have you brought us today?"

"We have freed more people from the slave ships. Do you think you can find more room for them?"

"Certainly, if they are willing to help build, there is room. How many do you have?"

"Nearly three hundred."

"Okay, and are you going to keep any for yourself?"

"No, I don't think so. I already have a full crew of Spaniards on my new ship."

"Then, we will find a place for everyone here."

As the people meandered along the beach, Raven called them together, speaking to them in Swahili. "I don't know where all of you people come from, but you are welcome to stay here. This is Shujaa wa Mfalme. He was once like you, a captive to be sold into slavery. I brought him here not long ago with many other people so they could start a new life together in freedom. If you decide not to stay, that is your concern, but I can take you no farther."

Some of the people began to cry out, "Why can't we go back to our villages?"

Mfalme raised his hands to quiet the crowd, "Please, please! You are not prisoners here. You may come and go as you please. However, if you decide to stay, you will be expected to contribute to the community. No one rides for free, as they say. If this is not suitable for you, there is the path over there. Take it and go. Or, you can take this path behind you, and it will take you to your new home, my village."

The people met in groups and debated what to do. Some began following the path heading east into the unknown, while the others followed the south path leading to Mfalme's village. Mfalme noticed an almost even split in the number of people traveling east and south.

He turned back to Raven and said, "I think they have made their choice."

Raven asked, "Do you need anything?"

Mfalme replied, "We can always use more tools for digging and building."

"I will bring more on my next visit."

"Thank you, Red Raven. Will you stay and feast with us tonight?"

"Not this time, Mfalme. I have a passenger who needs to get back to Ireland. I am on my way to Sekondi. He hopes to catch a ship from there to Ireland."

"I see. Well, you know you are always welcome here, Red Raven."

"Thank you, Mfalme. I will see you soon."

The two shook hands and parted ways. Raven returned to *Destiny* and found Sean waiting for her at the ship's rail.

"Is this where I will catch my next ship?"

"No, Sean. No ships come into port here other than mine. We will sail north to Sekondi, a Dutch settlement. You should be able to catch a ship back to England from there."

fi
Bogoso
Twifo Praso
R82
Damang
Prestea- Huni
Valley District
Kakum
National P
Tarkwa
N1
C
N1
Shama
Junction
Komenda
Sekondi-Takoradi
Takoradi
Agona
Dixcove
Gulf of Guinea

CHAPTER 9

Four days later, Raven's ship pulled into port at Sekondi. There were many ships in the harbor when they arrived. Most of them were being loaded with local timber that would be sailed to Holland for construction sites in cities like Rotterdam and The Hague. Raven thought Sean might be able to catch a ride on one of these ships.

The two ships pulled into port, flying white sails to avoid drawing too much attention. The harbor master directed them to two slips side by side where they could dock for a small fee. Raven thought she might dock *Destiny* and leave the *Sea Witch* in the harbor, but she realized this might be a good place to restock supplies.

Once they completed the docking process, Raven sent Jeffrey and Hadari ashore to restock the ships. Raven and Sean began searching for a ship with which he could travel to England. Raven carried a small leather pouch tied to her waist belt, in which she carried her money. She intended to buy Sean's passage back to Ireland if necessary.

The two walked down the boardwalk from ship to ship, asking to speak to each captain. Most of the vessels were Dutch cargo ships carrying timber back to Holland. Others were French vessels. Raven avoided those. She had no intention of ending up in a French prison again. The French government still wanted her for piracy. Two English vessels were parked at the docks, but neither was going directly back to England. After three hours of searching for a way to get Sean back to Ireland, Raven decided it was useless. So, she and Sean walked back to the ship.

When she returned, she found her men loading supplies onto both ships. Raven walked over to the *Sea Witch* to find Pharaoh. He stood on the quarterdeck, watching his men load the supplies onto the ship. When he saw Raven coming aboard, Pharaoh stepped down onto the main deck to meet her.

Raven said, "We had no luck finding a ship to carry Sean back to Ireland."

Pharaoh asked, "What do you intend to do then?"

"I was thinking we might split up. You take the *Sea Witch* and sail back to Port St. Felix: pick up more rum and anything else the mountain people might need so that we can trade for more gold. I'll take Sean and sail to Ireland. Maybe we can find a new market worth exploring while we're there."

Pharaoh replied, "Raven, you know I don't like it when we split up."

"I know, but you'll be fine. I have faith in you."

"It is not me I am worried about. It is you. If you go missing again, how will I know where to look for you?"

"Don't worry, Pharaoh. I'll be alright. I'll meet you back at the Robin's Nest in four to six weeks."

Begrudgingly, Pharaoh replied, "As you wish. I will see you in *four* weeks."

Raven wryly smiled, "Or five."

She left the *Sea Witch*, with Sean following behind. Raven then suggested, "Why don't you return to *Destiny* and wait for me there? I have more errands I want to make before we leave."

"Aye, young lassie. I'll be churnin' for yore return."

Sean walked over to *Destiny* and walked up the gangplank alone. Jeremy stood near the gangplank as Sean entered the ship. He asked, "Did you find a ship to take you to Ireland, Mr. O'Toole?"

"Nay, lad. But the young lass has agreed to take me there herself; she has."

Sean skipped away without a care.

Jeremy watched Raven as she turned down one of the side streets in front of *Destiny*. As he watched, he noticed two men following her down the street. No one else was on the street, which concerned Jeremy. Then, he saw one of the two take out a club and strike Raven across the back of her head. Jeremy gasped to witness his captain being assaulted. He turned to see who might be around to help.

"Mr. Ashworth!" he cried out. "Someone has just struck Raven!"

John, Jeffrey, and Attila jumped from the quarterdeck to lend aid to the captain. Jeremy followed them as they retreated from the ship and ran to help Raven. The two attackers were stuffing Raven into a burlap sack as fast as possible and didn't notice the four men brandishing weapons who were heading their direction.

Jeffrey was the first to arrive and struck one of the men across the back of his head with the hilt of his sword. John wielded a belaying pin and swung it at the other man, intent on tying the sack closed with Raven inside. John swung the pin, smashing the kidnapper across his nose, where blood and cracked bone mixed together. The man cried out, holding his face as he bent over, trying to collect himself. Jeremy and Attila took their turns striking either of the would-be kidnappers until both men lay on the ground unconscious and barely alive.

Jeffrey removed Raven from the sack and collected her in his arms. He carried her back to *Destiny* while the others escorted them back to safety. As they walked up the gangplank, John called over to Pharaoh, "We best get underway. Raven has been attacked, and the authorities may come looking for us."

Pharaoh waved his understanding and ordered his men to prepare to set sail. Attila did the same on *Destiny* while John and Jeffrey took Raven to her quarters. Jeremy escaped to the other end of the ship to retrieve Mr. Greer, the ship's doctor, to come to Raven's aid.

Andrew Greer collected his medical kit and raced to Raven's quarters. He pushed Jeffrey aside to look at the young woman he had treated many times before. He checked to see if she was breathing first. Satisfied she was, he checked the back of her skull to see what damage lay beneath the tangled, curly locks. Greer found a gash three inches long at the back of her head, but after pressing against her skull, he determined it was not cracked. He cleaned the wound as best he could and sewed the gash shut to stop the bleeding.

"What happened to her, John?" he asked.

"Jeremy saw two men trying to abduct her on the street. They clubbed her and stuffed her into a sack, trying to kidnap her."

Andrew asked, "What of the men? Are they alive?"

John replied, "I didn't wait to see. However, I doubt it after the beating they just received. Thus, the need for us to sail away with haste."

Attila stood on the quarterdeck, calling out orders, "All hands! Prepare for a quick departure! Cast off the bow line! Cast off the stern!"

The crew scrambled to their duties throughout the ship. Some climbed the rigging and unfurled the sails from the yardarm, while others released the ropes that tied the ship to the docks.

Attila checked the street where he and his cohorts had left the muggers. He witnessed two men moving down the street, finding the unconscious men lying in a pool of blood. The two looked around to see who might have committed the atrocity they saw before them. They called for help, and more citizens began running toward the beleaguered to see what was happening. Three men in uniform arrived and began to inspect the trouble. One of the local constables looked around to see who might have committed the crime of assault. One of the other constables remarked, "They're both dead."

Whistles blew, announcing a crime had been committed. More officers arrived to receive information on what to do. They all spread out to opposite points in the city to find a witness to the assault or the ones guilty of the two murders.

Raven's two ships sailed together, heading south until they were out of sight of the Dutch port. When they deemed it was safe, John called Pharaoh to come and moor beside him.

John asked, "Did you talk to Raven before she was attacked?"

"Aye, she said she would sail to Ireland to deliver Mr. O'Toole because they couldn't find a ship to take him. She told me to go to Port St. Felix to get another load of rum to trade with the mountain people. We were going to meet back at the Robin's Nest in four or six weeks."

John replied, "Alright, I see no reason not to follow that plan unless Raven gets worse."

"How is she?"

"She has a gash on the back of her skull, but Andrew says she didn't crack her skull, so she should be alright."

"That is good to hear. Do you know how she was injured?"

"Jeremy saw two men attack her as she was walking down the street. They were trying to kidnap her."

Pharaoh replied, "I hope they are dead."

"I'm pretty sure they are. They took enough of a beating to be."

Pharaoh nodded his approval, then stepped back from the rail to begin his flight to Madagascar.

"See you in six weeks!"

John waved as he turned and left.

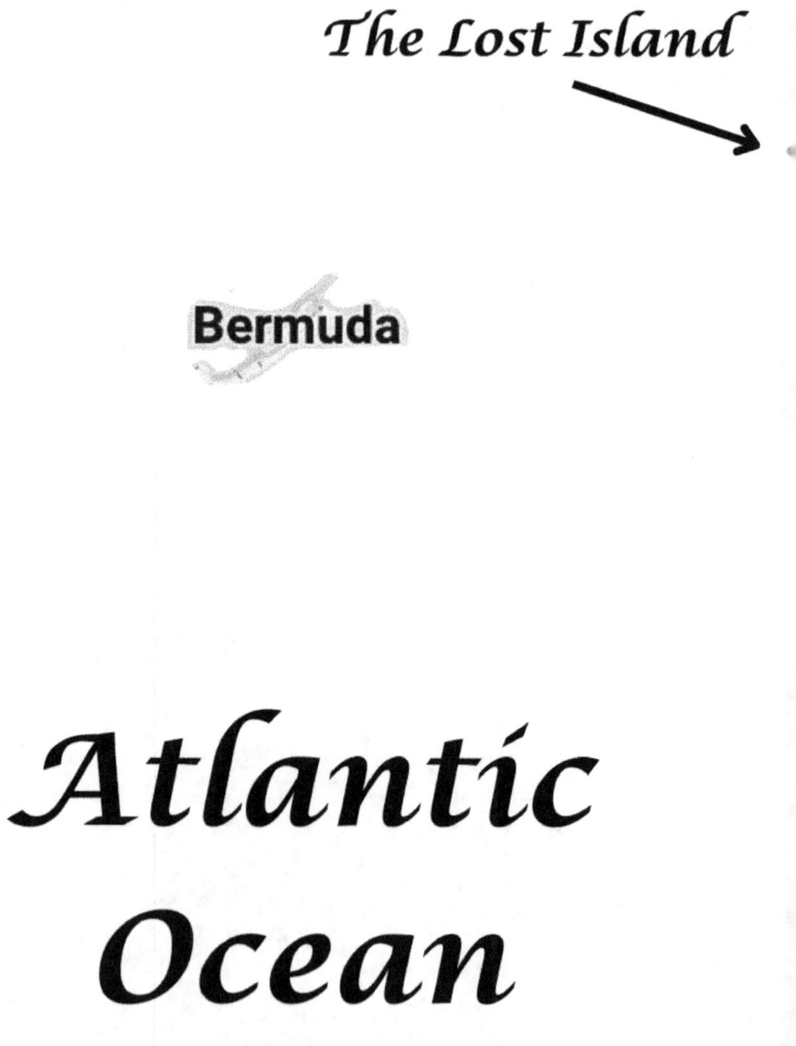

The Lost Island
Bermuda
Atlantic
Ocean

Chapter 10

The ship violently rocked and was tossed by the sea. Raven awoke as she heard Captain Billings fearfully squawk. She sat up in her bed and found someone had undressed her and laid her under the covers. Her head throbbed with each rocking movement the ship made as it bounced through what Raven felt must be a savage storm. She could hear the whistles and roars of the wind as it collided with *Destiny*.

Raven carefully stood and reached for her clothes. She wrapped her linen shirt around her before threading her arms through the sleeves and buttoning it down the front. She grabbed her leather britches and sat down so she could feed each leg into them and pull them up over her well-proportioned hips. Then she pulled her long boots on, found her long wool coat, and slid it on.

She attempted to walk to the door leading out of her cabin and into the hallway that led to the main deck. Raven stumbled across the floor, reaching for a chair, table, or wall; anything to help her maintain her balance. She felt intoxicated as she foundered along. As Raven turned the latch to open her hatch, the wind snatched the door from her grip, slamming it against the cabin wall. Rain propelled by wind soaked her face, stirring her from her grogginess. She stumbled out of her cabin, pulling the door behind her and securing it shut.

Raven heard muffled voices calling in the rain, but could not discern what they said. She gripped whatever wall was near as she crept across the deck. The skies were dark and gray, and there was no sun, moon, or stars to determine what time it might be. Raven eased to the quarterdeck and ascended the four steps leading to the helm.

John spied his daughter and stepped to her to steady her movements.

"What are you doing out of bed?" he asked.

"The storm awoke me!" she yelled back. "What time is it?"

"Believe it or not, it's nearly noon!"

Raven asked, "How long have I been out?"

"Four days!"

Raven asked, "Do you have any bearing on where we are?"

John replied, "The last time we caught a reading, we were two hundred miles west of Guinea. That was more than three hours ago. Our compass isn't working properly, and we can't get a reading from the sun or the stars because of the cloud cover. We think we're heading north, but who knows?"

Suddenly, lightning reached across the sky like a witch's outstretched claws. Over and over, the sky was lit up with the fiery display of electric energy. Raven and the others felt their hair stand on end with every bolt that flashed and struck against a sunless sky. Thunder roared like cannon fire with every lightning strike. The strikes came closer and closer as *Destiny* seemed to flail through the storm. Then, a lightning bolt struck the ship, knocking out its rudder. The wheel spun lifelessly in Kifaru's hands. *Destiny* was now at the mercy of the seas and God himself.

Destiny rocked even more violently through the waves since the crew no longer had any control over her. Raven instructed John, "We need to get those sheets up. They'll do us no good now and might do more harm if left unfurled."

John nodded and called out to the crew, "All sails up! All sails up!"

Jeremy sent his men into the rigging to climb to the yardarms and begin rolling up the sails and securing them. A young man named Jafaru walked across the yardarm and slipped. He fell thirty feet to the main deck and was instantly killed. Raven gasped as she witnessed the death of another one of her crew. Tears formed in the corners of her eyes, but mixed and mingled with the rain pelting her face.

Another of the crew called from the crow's nest, "I see a light 30º starboard!"

Raven looked into the distance and saw the sky wasn't clearing but changing color. The gray clouds gave way to a swirling blue mixed with pinks and oranges, much like a sunrise. The swirls moved in a circular pattern.

Raven asked, "Are those the Northern Lights?"

John replied, "I don't know. I have never been far enough north to see the Northern Lights. I don't see how we could be far enough to the north now to see them."

Raven asked, "Then what is it?"

The rain suddenly ceased. The clouds still hovered over them but began to roll away from one another, creating a vortex before them. *Destiny*, without the aid of sail or paddle, was suddenly drawn into the path of the vortex. First, the ship moved forward into the wake of the swirling columns of clouds. Then, she picked up speed like no other ship had ever sailed. Raven and her crew held on for their lives as the ship approached 60, then 70 knots. Raven held onto the rail at the edge of the quarterdeck as the wind picked up, blowing stronger and stronger.

The ship bounced on top of the sea, sometimes feeling like it was flying out of the water. Raven's eyes widened with fear as their speed continued to increase. Then, a funnel appeared in the distance, swirling in the water, churning and spinning clockwise. *Destiny* was captured in the cyclonic force, spinning her around the edge of the funnel in a dizzying fashion. Many of her crew were left hanging for their lives from the ship's rigging as the *Destiny* swirled through the funnel of waves. John and the others, standing on the quarterdeck, knelt next to the rail and held on, trying not to be tossed overboard by the centrifugal force of the spinning ship.

Everyone's heads spun as they tried to ride out the forces holding them captive. The spinning and speed increased more and more until it was unbearable. Raven's head began to throb, her stomach started churning, and she thought she might vomit even though she hadn't eaten in four days. Then, she blacked out.

Raven awoke, finding herself still lying on the quarterdeck. Her clothes were soaked as she raised herself to stand next to the rail. As she looked around, she saw John and the others beginning to awaken as well.

She strode over to John and called to him, "Papa? Papa, are you alright?"

John shook his head and replied, "I, I think so, daughter. Where are we?"

Raven looked around, seeing her crew throughout the ship coming back to consciousness, except the ones who had fallen from the rigging and were now dead. She saw Jeremy making his way from body to body, checking the ones who had not yet awakened. They were all dead. Raven counted; eight men lay lifeless on the ship's deck.

Raven looked across the railing to see where they might be. She checked the compass and saw the needle spinning out of control. Although she had no idea whether it was morning or afternoon, she checked the sun to see its location. She spun around and found it behind her; only it had a strange glow that she had never witnessed before. It looked like its color had changed from a blinding yellow to an almost moldy green.

She looked below it and saw a shimmering wave that appeared to reveal an island. Raven scanned the horizon all around her and realized it was the only land in sight. She called to Jeremy and ordered, "Get all four dories in the water! We need to pull *Destiny* to that island aft of us."

Jeremy replied, "Aye, Raven!"

Jeremy sent four crews of four into the sea at the ship's bow, each attached to the ship with a tug line. Four men on each dory pulled against an oar, trying to move the ship forward. They seemed to be going nowhere, just pushing water away from the little boats but gaining no distance.

Jeremy ordered, "Pull together! Spread out away from each other and give yourselves room to work!"

The boats moved away from one another until they were about twenty feet apart. They began to row together as one of the men called out a cadence to the others. They worked together and found they were creating momentum that caused *Destiny* to move. They only initially moved an inch or two, but then they began increasing in speed.

Jeremy ordered, "Alright, now let's swing her starboard! Port oars only!"

Each man holding the oar on the port side of the dories kept rowing while the other rowers rested. *Destiny* turned.

After a while, Jeremy called again, "Now, together once more!"

Four oars on each boat were pulled through the waters again to straighten out the dories so they could spread apart once again. Jeremy had them pull the port side only again. Jeremy continued to move the dories so that they could make their way to the island Raven had seen.

Slowly, the island grew as they approached it from the sea. It was larger than Raven had first expected. It seemed to widen as they rowed closer. A large mountain rose from the middle and extended toward the green sun. A thin line of smoke emitted from the top of the mountain. Raven thought she could see birds gliding around the top edge.

They continued forward, moving slowly but surely now. Raven thought she saw a pod of pelicans flying toward the ship, but they didn't seem to be flying together in a V-formation as they usually would. As they approached, Raven could see they were not white or gray like she had expected. They were darker—a dark leathery brown.

One of the creatures broke away from the pod and sailed toward the ship. It screamed out at the approaching vessel with a most disturbing cry. Raven noted that it sounded like metal scraping against metal, only louder than any sound she had ever heard anywhere. She, too, noticed it had no feathers.

"Is that some kind of bat?"

John replied, "I have never seen anything like it. It's gigantic!"

The creature continued its path toward the ship, gliding about 100 feet above the water's surface. As it came closer, they could see finger-like protrusions on the front of its wings. Unlike the pelican, it also had a row of teeth lining its bill on top and bottom. It screamed again with an ear-piercing cry and dipped toward the water near the dories.

Those who were pulling the oars saw the creature moving toward them. They panicked, watching it come closer and directly at their boats. It dived at the group's dory farthest starboard, and men began diving into the sea to avoid its open jaws. It was as large as two dories lying side by side. The winged creature swooped toward the dories and caught one of the crew in its talons. Then, it stretched back into the open sky with the man screaming in terror. Blood dripped into the sea as the creature flew back toward the island.

Raven watched as it flew away and saw more creatures flying toward the first. One of them attacked the creature, which still held the man in its clutches. They tangled together in the sky as they wrestled to see who would come away with the fresh meal. Raven, horrified, witnessed her man as he was torn in half by the two creatures.

CHAPTER 11

Raven felt anger and fear as she saw him split between the ravenous, featherless birds. She turned to her crew and called, "Man, the guns! All hands, man, the guns!"

Any crew still on board moved to the cannons and loaded them while the officers took up long rifles. The cannons were loaded with canister shots and prepared for any approaching attacks. The canister shot would spread out multiple smaller cannonballs at its target like a shotgun. With no rudder available to help them maneuver, Raven had to depend on luck that the creatures might fly into the path of one of her cannons.

Raven commanded, "Fire at will!"

Jeremy stood at the cannon closest to the quarterdeck on the starboard side, waiting for one of the creatures to fly into his path. The shot would be difficult because of the elevation factor involved. Jeremy knew that luck would play a massive part in his ability to hit one of the leather-bound birds.

A pod of twenty flew toward the ship, sensing that a meal could be had on the vessel, which floundered in the water. Jeremy waited for the right moment and yelled, "Fire!"

A shot rang out, sending multiple tiny cannonballs into the air. The creatures screeched as the metal pellets struck them. One of the creatures had a projectile rip through one of its wings, causing it to falter in flight, so it fell into the sea. Another was struck in the head and knocked unconscious so that it, too, fell into the open waters. Several other creatures saw their fellows fall into the sea and dove toward the water, not to save the companions but to feed on them. A feeding frenzy broke out as the remaining creatures dove in for the free meal.

Raven and the others watched as the winged reptiles fell in on each other and fought for survival. Since they could not swim, they struggled against each other and the water. Blood filled the ocean as more creatures arrived to participate in the frenzy.

Raven saw it as a chance to escape, "Get back into the boats! Get us out of here!"

Her crew, treading in the water, swam back to the boats and climbed back into them. They rowed again, trying to get *Destiny* as far away from the creatures as possible. Raven knew the island was not ideal for them to moor against after witnessing the danger it had already presented to her, but they had little choice. They had to find a way to repair their rudder if they were going to escape this unknown perilous place.

The crew continued to row while Jeremy and his gunners watched over them. No more of the featherless creatures approached them, and the ones that had attempted to snatch them from the sea were now dying in the depths of the water, either by other members of their own species or by the many sharks that had now arrived, searching for the source of blood which they had sensed.

Raven stared up into the sky once more to see if she could determine what time of day it was. As they approached the island, she saw the green sun had moved little as they had struggled to reach the island. However, the sky around the expansive mountain in the middle of the island had changed. Not only was there a column of smoke rising from the mountain-top, but a cloud ring was forming and expanding around the area where the mountain stood. A black rolling cloud hovered over the mountain, spinning around like a carousel.

Birds could be heard as the ship floated closer to the island. Panicked, they flew away from the mountain to the trees at the outermost part of the island. They flew to the treetops at the edge of the beaches, removing themselves as far away as possible from the thunderous rumblings of the mountain without leaving the island.

When *Destiny* reached the shore, Raven had her crew drop anchor about 50 yards from the beach. She had one of the dories row to the ship's aft to examine the rudder. Mtu Mdago was sitting in the boat's bow as it approached *Destiny's* rudder, or what was left of it. Mdago sat in the boat as he peered into the compartment where the rudder rested. He could see that the steerage ropes were frayed and broken, but after closer examination, he also saw that the rudder had been smashed. Everything would have to be rebuilt and replaced before they could expect to leave this uncharted island.

"Raven! It is not good. We will have to start from scratch. The rudder is completely destroyed."

"I'll let Mr. Greer know so he can get started removing the old rudder. Have everyone come back onboard for now."

"Aye, Raven."

The four dory crews climbed back onboard the ship and reloaded the dories back onto the ship. Raven walked to Andrew Greer's cabin to discuss the repairs *Destiny* would need to undergo. As she entered the infirmary, she found Mr. Greer attending to two of the men who had been injured during the storm. One had a broken left arm from falling from the lowest yardarm of the foremast. The other man was unconscious, lying on a bed. He had hit his head on the deck when the ship lunged sideways during the storm.

"Mr. Greer, when you have a moment, we need to discuss *Destiny's* repairs."

"How much damage did she sustain?"

"Our rudder was destroyed along with all the steerage ropes. Do we have enough timber to make a new rudder?"

"No, Raven, I'm afraid not. Are we near an island where we can harvest timber to do the job?"

"We've just anchored near a beach on an island that might have suitable trees, but it also has what appears to be a volcano in the middle, ready to erupt."

"If you can have Simba come and look after these two, I'll go and look to see if we can find what we need to make the repairs."

Raven replied, "I'll do that."

She turned and left the infirmary and called Simba, who was helping bring the dories back onboard. When Simba met Raven near the forecastle, Raven instructed her, "Go and relieve Mr. Greer in the infirmary so he can oversee the ship's repairs."

"Aye, Raven."

When Andrew met Raven on the main deck, the two descended to the lower deck and walked to the stern to look closer at the ship's steerage. As they walked together, ducking their heads to miss the cross beams that held up the main deck, Raven was reminded of her first days serving alongside Mr. Greer, learning the jobs of the ship's carpenter and doctor. She had learned so much from Mr. Greer those first years onboard the original *Destiny*. She spent as much free time as she could reading his medical journals. It now seemed like it had been a lifetime ago.

When they reached the steering compartment at the ship's rear, Andrew observed that the remaining part of the rudder was in splinters. The rope that moved the rudder by way of the ship's wheel was in several pieces.

"I hope we have enough rope to replace this one," Greer commented.

Raven replied, "If not, maybe the *Sea Witch* has some onboard we can use."

Raven realized she had not seen the *Sea Witch* since the storm began. Her countenance fell as she realized her other ship was missing.

"Do what you can, Mr. Greer. I need to speak to Papa."

"Aye."

Raven walked through the lower deck until she found the upward ladder. She climbed up and then almost ran to the quarterdeck.

"Papa? Have you seen the *Sea Witch*?"

John also realized he hadn't seen the other ship since the storm began.

"No, Raven, I haven't."

She turned away and asked anyone within hearing distance, "Has anyone seen the *Sea Witch*?"

The only responses she received were blank stares and headshakes. Raven took out her spyglass and searched the horizon for any sign of the missing ship. Her stomach churned with anxiety as she realized she may have lost two of her oldest friends to the recent storm. "*Maybe they were just taken off course,*" she thought.

Dread filled her heart as she remembered all those she had lost over the past year. She didn't think she could stand losing anyone else, especially Pharaoh and Alexander. Pharaoh had been with Raven since she was twelve and Alexander since she was thirteen.

Raven asked John, "Papa, what should we do? We don't know where we are or where the *Sea Witch* is."

"Well, Raven, the first thing we need to do is repair our rudder so we can get back out to sea and find the *Sea Witch*."

"Right. Of course. We don't have enough timber onboard to make the repairs. We'll need to send a crew onto the island to find enough proper wood to build a new rudder. Papa, I need you to stay on board. I'll take Attila with me. We will search for suitable trees to cut for our new rudder."

"How long will you be gone?"

"Hopefully, not more than three days; five at the most."

John wrinkled his face, "I don't like it, daughter. This doesn't seem to be like any other island we have explored. Who knows what might be waiting for you out there?"

"I know, Papa. But what choice do we have? We won't be going any-where until we can repair *Destiny*."

"Let me go instead."

"No, Papa. I won't endanger you or anyone else unless I'm there with you. I need someone here on the ship who can command should I not return. I trust no one more than you."

Raven gathered her exploration crew together on the deck of the ship. Jeffery, Attila, Hadari, Kujana wa Muziki, Kifaru, Mtu Mdago, Mwanamke Mtamu, Mvuvi, Bila Meno, Simba, and Seremala came along armed with swords, pistols, and axes. Raven and Simba were the only women coming along, yet they were also the most skilled fighters among the crew.

They took two dories to the beach and secured them to palm trees at the forest's edge. Everyone looked around warily as they began to trek through the jungle. Hadari took the lead, hacking through the foliage blocking their path. Raven noted the smells of the island as they followed Hadari. Sulfur entered Raven's nostrils as she looked in every direction. Some of the plant life was familiar, but their aspects were wrong. Pine cones, the size of watermelons, lay on the jungle floor. Lilies stood seven feet tall with blossoms the size of dinner plates. Insects buzzed all around them with almost deafening songs.

Kifaru asked, "Raven, why can't we use one of these trees to get timber for the rudder?"

"Because pine is too soft. We need hardwood like oak, poplar, or mahogany."

"What if this island doesn't have any of those?"

"Then and only then will I settle for the pine. But if we can find hardwood, I would rather have that.

After an hour of trudging through the forest, Hadari led them into a small clearing about twenty feet in diameter. Raven said, "Let's take a break."

They all sat on the ground, which was covered with a carpet of moss and pine needles spread out over the sand. They passed around water skins and rested as the insects continued singing their welcome songs.

Suddenly, Raven realized a new smell. She looked around where she sat and found a large mound of dung.

"Oh, my! That's terrible. What creature could have possibly made that?"

Hadari remarked, "It is the wrong shape, but it is as large as an elephant would produce. But the smell is much worse."

Raven got up and found a new place to sit. A rustle came from the foliage behind her as soon as she sat down. Startled, Raven rose again, pulled out her sword, and waited.

CHAPTER 12

Three men stumbled out of the jungle. She thought the one in the lead was about thirty years old, clean-shaven, tall, and good-looking. The second man was helping a third man who was injured. They all wore matching khaki-colored clothing as if part of some military group, but the clothing was strange and unfamiliar to Raven.

The two following burst into the clearing and fell to the ground from exhaustion. The leader stood before them as if to protect them, holding only a strange-looking pistol. The leader swung around in the center of the clearing, pointing his weapon at anyone who moved.

"Who are you, people?"

He spoke English but spoke with a strange dialect.

Raven stepped forward and replied, "I am the Red Raven; these are my crew. Who are you?"

The leader asked, "What? Are you on your way to a costume party or something? Where did you get those outfits?"

Raven lifted her sword and said, "I told you who we are, sir. Now, tell me who you are."

"I'm Lieutenant Charles Taylor of the United States Naval Reserve out of Corpus Christi, Texas, and these are my flight crew."

Raven was confused by the words she had just heard: *United States, flight crew*. These were unfamiliar terms to her.

"Well, Leftenant, your speech is unfamiliar to me. What is a United States Naval Reserve?"

"I'm in the reserve navy. I'm not full-time. I was called into service when the war broke out."

"What war might that be?"

"World War 2!" he replied.

"World War 2? Shouldn't there first be a World War 1 before we have a World War 2?"

"There was. It ended in 1918."

Raven furrowed her brow, "1918? What year do you think it is now?"

"1945, of course. What year did you think it was?" he chuckled.

"The year is 1708."

Taylor stood with his mouth agape. Then he looked at his dumbfounded men.

"Leftenant?"

"Please, call me Charles."

"Of course, Charles. What year do you think it is?"

"1945."

"And, what is the United States?"

"United States! It's the United States of America. That's our country. Corpus Christi is my city, and Texas is my state. Corpus Christi, Texas, of the United States of America."

"Where is your country located?"

"Ah, yes, of course. You probably know it as the American colonies."

Raven asked, "You mean the Carolinas?"

"Yes, the Carolinas are just a part of the United States now. Forty-eight states make up the United States."

"So, the King of England rules over these 48 states?"

"No, America won its independence in 1776. Well, it was 1783 before we were allowed our independence."

Raven mused, "Hmm, that's interesting. So, Charles, how did you get on this island in the year 1708?"

"Well, I'm not sure. I'm not even sure it is 1708. It could be anytime. We were on a bomber exercise on our way to Bermuda from Fort Lauderdale, Florida. On returning to Florida, we ran into a strange storm that caused our instruments to go haywire."

"Haywire?"

"Uh, bonkers?"

"Oh, right. Continue."

"We lost our engine and had to bail out of the ship."

"How did water get into your ship? From the storm?"

"No, it's not a sea vessel; it's a flying ship."

"In the air? A ship that flies in the air? Well, how did the water get into your flying ship?"

"No, it wasn't water that was being bailed out. We were bailing out. We jumped out of the ship before it crashed."

"Oh, my. Well, you must not have been flying all that high to have come out of it unscathed."

"No, we had parachutes. It's like sails on your ship. The parachute catches the wind as we fall through the sky and slows down our momentum so we can safely land on the ground."

"Oh my, my, my! Are you hearing this, Jeffrey?"

Jeffrey smiled and nodded his agreement.

Raven realized she had not introduced everyone.

"Pardon me, Leftenant Charles, this is Jeffrey Hamilton, my quartermaster."

Then she pointed out the others, "This is one of my captains, Attila, my second mate, Hadari, and the rest of my crew, or at least the ones who came ashore with me."

"Pleased to meet y'all. These are my men, George Devin and Walter Parpart."

Charles asked, "Are you all in the British Navy?"

Raven giggled, "Oh my, no! We're pirates."

Charles was shocked again. "Pardon me, Captain, but you don't look like a pirate. Excuse me for saying so, but you are much too beautiful to be a pirate."

"Haven't you ever heard that looks can be deceiving?"

"Yes, of course. Please excuse my ignorance. So, what are you doing on this island? Are you searching for treasure?"

"No, we're searching for timber. The storm damaged our rudder, and we need to find some suitable wood to replace it. By the way, what's the matter with your man there?"

"He's got a gash on his leg. We can't get it to quit bleeding. He probably needs stitches."

"Let me have a look."

Raven approached the injured man and asked, "What was your name?"

"Walter Parpart, miss. You can just call me Walt."

"Alright, Walt. Let's have a look."

Walt was much younger than the lieutenant. Raven thought maybe he was her age, so she asked.

"How old are you, Walt?"

"Nineteen, miss."

"Well, you and I are close to the same age. I just turned twenty."

Raven unwrapped Walt's leg and exposed a gash about four inches long, still bleeding. Raven reached into her satchel and pulled out her medical kit. She took a small bottle of alcohol and flushed the wound. Walt winced as the alcohol burned. Raven removed a needle and horse hair to suture the wound shut. She wrapped it with a cotton bandage and deemed him ready to go. Walt gingerly stood on his leg, and with George's help, they walked with Raven's group as they paraded through the jungle.

A bird chattered nearby as it witnessed the group trudging through its territory. Another bird, possibly a woodpecker, hammered against a tree off to their right, and the hammering echoed throughout the forest.

Hadari halted everyone by raising his fist. Everyone stood quietly along the path. Hadari pointed off to his right. Something was moving through the brush, coming toward them. Raven signaled for everyone to hide in the foliage along the newly cut trail. They watched as something crossed in front of Hadari. Not just one, but a column of them. Ants marched past them. Ants the size of a medium-sized dog. Red, with jaws that opened horizontally instead of vertically, like a human. Antennas stood on top of their heads, moving around above them as they walked. The lead insect stopped in the path of the human intruders as if listening or smelling for something unusual. Hadari held his finger to his mouth to quiet everyone.

The lead ant lost interest in whatever it had noticed and proceeded down its path. Hadari stood and quietly moved forward. He looked to his left in the direction the ants had taken, then moved without cutting a trail. Everyone followed, although it was more difficult without Hadari cutting a path. Seremala, the last one in line, heard something behind him. He turned and saw a lonely stray ant looking at him. Seremala drew his sword and faced the ant while loudly whispering to the others, "Hey! We've been spotted!"

One by one, Raven's group stopped to see what was the matter at the back of the line. The ant stood on the pathway, looking at the strange human standing before him. His antenna began violently swinging, swaying, and circling his head. Suddenly, another ant's head popped out from around the corner of the path. Then another. Seremala shouted to everyone, "Run! They are coming! Run!"

Everyone began yelling in line until the message reached Hadari, "Run! Run! Run!"

Hadari swung his blade against the vegetation, but not fast enough for them to escape the ants. The ants came at them, clicking their horizontal jaws, ready to take a bite out of the intruders. Together, the clicking was so loud that no one could hear the others talk. Seremala swung his sword at the nearest one, slicing through its head and killing it. However, the death of one seemed only to anger the others as they swarmed around Seremala instantaneously, knocking him to the ground.

No one could hear the young African as he cried for help. The ants' vise-like jaws ripped Seremala apart before Raven's eyes, and she stood stunned, realizing another of her men had fallen victim to one of her blunders. Hadari grabbed Raven's arm and led her away while the others fought for their lives.

They returned to the little clearing and lined up to make a stand against the giant insects. Taylor pulled out a revolver from his gun belt and fired six times, striking a different ant each time. George and Walter did the same, leaving eighteen dead ants on the ground before them. Raven and her men were stunned as they saw the sailors using the weapons that fired multiple rounds without reloading. But they regained their composure, slashed at the remaining ants with their blades, and fired with their one-shot pistols. Legs, antennas, and heads fell to the wayside as they fought for their lives. Several of the insects decided the battle was futile. They turned and ran away from the intruders.

Raven's group gathered in the clearing to regain their composure. They sat together in small groups to rest as they heard the ants moving away in the opposite direction. Raven turned to Charles Taylor and asked, "What kind of weapons are those?"

"This is a .38 Special Victory revolver made by Smith and Wesson."

"How is it that you can fire so many shots without reloading?"

Taylor handed her the weapon to examine as he explained, "The revolver uses cartridges that load into these cylinder chambers."

Taylor handed Raven a new cartridge as he continued, "You load six of these cartridges into the cylinder, then slide the cylinder shut. Pull back this hammer and pull the trigger to shoot. Each time you pull back the hammer, the cylinder revolves, moving the next cartridge in line with the hammer. Do you see that tiny percussion cap at the base of the cartridge? The hammer hits that, which ignites the gunpowder inside the cartridge, making the bullet move through the gun's barrel."

Raven asked, "Does everyone carry weapons like this in your time?"

"Military and police carry them, or at least similar weapons. But most folks don't carry weapons in my time. At least, not the civilized people."

"Is this what you use in your flying ship to shoot at the enemy?"

"No, we use a .30 caliber machine gun. It can fire much faster and make more shots than the handgun."

"How many more?"

"It can fire between 1200 -1500 shots per minute."

"What?! How can it be?"

"I don't know how it works, exactly. George is the gunner. I just fly the plane."

"Will wonders never cease?"

Raven gathered everyone, and they trekked back into the forest in search of the timber needed to repair their ship. Lieutenant Taylor and his men tagged along, not wanting to be alone in this new and dangerous world. He was delighted to have met the young sea captain and her crew from another time and another place, but he didn't like the idea of being stranded in a place and time not of his own.

Chapter 13

Hadari was back to hacking his way through the forest. The vegetation was nothing like he had ever seen before. Flowering plants towered over him. The pale yellow blossoms seemed to follow his every move. As Hadari moved forward, the flower followed his movement. The same if he stepped backward.

He turned to Attila and asked, "Did you see that?"

"What?"

"The flower, it follows me wherever I move."

Hadari demonstrated for Attila.

Attila remarked, "That is strange."

Everyone in line became aware of the blossoms as they walked down the freshly cut trail. The flowers seemed to watch them as they walked past, changing from person to person. Raven reached out to touch one of the blossoms, but it repelled away from her touch.

Raven turned to Taylor, who was following her, and said, "What an odd place this is."

"Yes, it is."

A new flowering plant appeared as Hadari continued trudging and cutting through the jungle. The stalk of the flower was over six feet tall; its blossom was star-shaped with several pistils in the center. The colors of the flowers ranged from deep purples to light pinks. Hadari hacked through the stem of one of the flowers, clearing a pathway. The flower's pistils shot out from the center of the plant, flying through the air. One of the pistils hit Hadari on the right side of his neck. He swatted at his neck, thinking an insect had bitten him. He swiped away the pistil and continued hacking through the vegetation. After a while, Hadari became dizzy. He began sweating profusely, and his eyes rolled back in his head before he fell backward and passed out.

Attila reached him first and called his name, "Hadari! Hadari, wake up!"

Raven rushed forward to see what was the matter.

"What happened to him?"

"I don't know. He just passed out suddenly."

Raven began to look Hadari over, searching for any signs of injury. She found a spot on the right side of his neck, swollen and red with a pin-sized hole in the skin.

"It looks like he's been stung."

Attila asked, "Will he be alright?"

"I don't know. I hope so, but this place is like none other we have ever seen. I have no idea what dangers lie amongst these plants and insects. Let's get someone up here to clear the path for us and someone to carry Hadari."

Attila called back to the back of the line, "Muziki! Mdago! Mvuvi! Come forward."

The three men came forward to receive their orders.

"Muziki, continue cutting the trail for us, but be careful where you swing the machete. Mdago and Mvuvi, pick up Hadari and bring him along."

The men did as they were ordered, and the group continued through the jungle. Attila followed Muziki as he cut the trail, with Mdago and Mvuvi following. They dragged Hadari between them as each man draped one of Hadari's arms around their shoulders. The trail was too narrow for them to move abreast, though, without touching the surrounding wall of vegetation. Mdago rubbed against one of the star-shaped flowers, and the flower spat out more pistils. Luckily, they shot over his head and missed him.

Raven saw what happened and said, "Be careful; those plants shoot out something like little darts. That might be what struck Hadari and caused him to pass out."

As Musiki continued cutting through the forest, he eventually found a patch of plants resembling dandelions. The pillowy tops of the dandelions appeared like any other he had seen, but the flowers stood three feet tall. Without much thought, Musiki struck a patch of the flowers, causing the seeds to float through the air like dandelions often do. However, several of the seeds landed on Attila's bare arm, and his skin burned. Attila swiped away the seeds and yelped his discontent.

"Be careful! Those dandelion seeds burn your skin!"

Those walking behind Attila paused and waited for the seeds to fly away from the path before continuing on the pathway behind Attila and Muziki. When they felt the path was clear, they began their trek once more. However, as the men carrying Hadari passed through, they rubbed against the dandelions, causing a horrendous storm of seeds to scatter throughout the air around them. It was as if one flower received a signal from another plant, and they passed it on to the next plant. Suddenly, the air was filled with the stinging seeds.

There was nowhere for Raven and her crew to hide. The seeds attacked them without mercy, stinging any exposed skin they could touch. Luckily, most of Raven's skin was covered by clothing except for the area around her face, neck, and hands. Most of the Africans, however, were bare-chested and wearing cut-off pants. Each of them received sting after sting and burn after burn as the flower seeds floated around them. There was nothing they could do to prevent or ward off their attackers. They had to press on through the pain as they passed through.

The farther Raven's crew traveled toward the island's center, the more pungent the stench of sulfur grew in their nostrils. The vegetation was too tall to see where the mountain at the center of the island stood anymore, and without a working compass, they could only guess which way they should travel. Raven looked to the sky to find where the sun might be, but it was hidden by the circling dark clouds above. The light of day grew dimmer and dimmer as Muzuki hacked his way through the vegetation.

Large insects the size of rats scurried across their path. They appeared to be similar to the cock roaches Raven had seen at Port St. Felix on the island of Madagascar, but these were much larger. Raven drew her cutlass and stabbed one of the creatures as it scurried past her. The bug popped, expelling a gruesome yellow ooze from its body.

Hundreds of the insects appeared on the path, running toward the dead roach. Raven let out a yelp as thousands of roaches ran in her direction. She stabbed over and over, killing at least one with every plunge of her blade. It seemed that the more she killed, the more came running at her. Simba came to Raven's aid, plunging her spear at the large bugs and killing them as quickly as she could, but killing the bugs just seemed to bring more in their direction.

Raven yelled to the front of the line, "Get us out of here!"

Muzuki slashed with all his stamina, leading them away from the grizzly scene. Everyone kept stabbing at the roaches, but more and more appeared from the jungle as they did.

"Don't kill anymore! I think that's what is attracting them to us. Leave them alone and get out of here!"

Everyone followed, trying to abide by Raven's orders, but as they continued down the path, there was no way to get past the creatures without stepping on them, killing more of them, and attracting more to their location.

There were so many bugs that they began climbing over each other and up the legs of Raven and her explorers. Raven became disconcerted by the giant bugs crawling up her legs. She and the others tried to brush them off as they ran away from the resilient roaches.

Muziki gave up trying to cut a path and ran as quickly through the brush as he could, with everyone following behind. However, running through the jungle triggered the reflexes of the dangerous plants growing in their path. Stamen, pistils, and pollen filled the air around them as they passed through the jungle's overgrowth.

The trekkers sneezed uncontrollably as they ran through the jungle. They swiped away at the tiny darts that pierced their bodies, stinging with excessive pain. Still, they couldn't stop; they ran as fast as possible, tripping over their feet and one another.

Then, a new sound filled their ears. Bluebirds the size of eagles appeared from nowhere. Thousands of them filled the jungle, where the roaches were feeding on their dead companions. The birds dove to the ground, plucked the bugs from the earth, and flew back into the air to swallow their prey. The birds swirled through the air, climbing and diving back to the ground, filling their bellies with the giant bugs until none were left.

Muzuki continued through the jungle, hacking a path as best he could. His strength was waning. The stings from the plant pistils began to take their toll on his body and those following him down the path. Luckily, the path opened up into a small clearing behind a freshwater stream. The crew all bound into the clearing and sank their faces into the cool, clear water of the stream. The toxins of the pistils took over, and everyone fell asleep.

Hadari was the first to awaken. Although he woke to complete darkness, he could tell others were lying near him. He heard the stream that flowed nearby and crawled in that direction. Hadari balked when he felt the first body in his path. Whoever it was, they were wearing unfamiliar clothing. The shirt was made of a material Hadari had never felt before. He continued to crawl and eventually reached the stream. He dipped his face into the water and allowed it to wash over his face. Hadari gulped the water until he was quenched.

Hadari heard a rumble nearby. Not a rumble, a growl. He couldn't see anything, but he knew whatever it was could see him. He fumbled through his satchel, which was still hanging around his neck, and found his fire flint and a knife. He felt around on the ground, searching for anything that could be used as tender. Hadari scraped together a small pile of dried leaves, grass, and anything else he thought might burn quickly. He raked his knife across the flint, causing sparks to fly into the tiny pile of tinder.

The growling grew closer as he struggled to start the fire. Hadari began to sweat, not only because of the effort needed to start the fire but also because of the looming danger he hoped to avoid by starting the fire.

A small flame ignited, and a tiny column of smoke began to rise from the tender. Hadari bent over and blew toward the tiny flame, trying to coax it into a much larger one. Finally, *puff!* The fire flamed up, creating light enough to illuminate the clearing where his friends lay unconscious.

Hadari hastily fed the flame, letting it grow more and more, and adding more significant pieces of wood to the flames.

The growls increased in number and intensity. Hadari kept watch against the edge of the clearing, searching for the source of the growls. As he gathered more wood for the fire, he also picked up weapons from his companions, who slept unaware of the danger, moving toward them. He collected every pistol he could find and tossed them into a pile near the fire. He gathered a collection of cutlasses and stood them up around him by stabbing them into the sand. Then, he waited.

Orange eyes began to appear against the backdrop of the forest. First, one pair, then another, and another until Hadari counted ten pairs of eyes piercing the darkness. The growls intensified as the creatures moved closer to the clearing. Hadari picked up two pistols and braced himself for what was to come.

CHAPTER 14

One of the creatures stepped out into the clearing, bearing its teeth as it continued to growl. Hadari saw that the creature was enormous, about the size of a full-grown male lion. But it looked more like a dog or a hyena, only hairless. Its skin looked pinkish in the firelight. The menacing eyes, no longer glowing, had turned black.

More and more of the dog-like creatures exposed themselves to the light of the clearing. They took their time approaching the single man standing between them and the free meal lying beside the stream.

Hadari glanced down and saw Jeffrey lying next to where he knelt. He shook Jeffrey's body, trying to rouse him from his deep sleep.

"Jeffrey! Jeffrey, wake up!"

Hadari reached down and felt for a pulse in Jeffrey's neck. He wasn't dead, only asleep and unwilling or unable to wake. Hadari tried another lying nearby. It was Simba.

"Simba! Wake up, Simba!"

She also would not awaken.

The creatures weren't patient. They were ready to eat, but only one man stood in their way. The first one leaped at Hadari from eight feet away. Hadari raised the pistol in his right hand and fired, hitting the animal in the chest. It fell short of Hadari, unable to move, but another took its place, leaping at the stranger. Hadari raised the pistol in his left hand and fired. **Boom!**

The shot missed, and the creature landed on Hadari with its jaws opened and ready for the first taste of flesh. Hadari used the animal's momentum to roll backward, flipping the animal over and away from him. He grabbed another pistol from the pile and fired again, this time hitting the creature in the head, killing it instantly.

Hadari whirled around, ready for the next attack. He saw one of the creatures dragging someone away. He picked up another pistol and fired, hitting the creature's shoulder, wounding it, and causing it to yelp like a whipped puppy.

Hadari knelt by the pile of pistols, firing continually at his attackers coming from all directions until he had spent every load. Eight creatures lay wounded or dead in the clearing. Two remained, and Hadari had no time to reload his weapons.

He drew a cutlass from the sand where he had left them. He approached the remaining attackers as they circled him. Hadari swung his right cutlass at the beast on his right, missing. The beast on his left saw an opening and lunged at him. Hadari blocked the animal using his left cutlass against its jaws as the creature rolled him to the ground. The other beast grabbed Hadari's right arm and began tugging it with such force that Hadari thought his arm might be separated from his body.

"Ahh!" He screamed in pain as the creature's teeth clamped into His flesh.

Hadari managed to get a foot into the belly of the creature on his left and pushed against the beast, tossing it away temporarily. He swung his left saber at the animal on his right arm and struck it in the shoulder, slicing an eight-inch gash in the creature's hairless hide. The beast never let go of Hadari's arm. He continued to hack at the animal as fast as possible, sometimes causing injury and sometimes missing.

The beast on Hadari's left regained its composure and leaped toward him. **Boom!** A shot rang out from behind Hadari, and he saw his attacker fall to the ground and die.

He continued hacking at the beast on his right arm until, **Boom!** Another shot rang out and killed the creature. Hadari lay still, panting in the sand, tears dripping from his eyes. The muscles in his right arm ached from the mangled mess the creature had left him with.

Hadari lay in the sand with his eyes closed, trying to ignore the agony of his injuries. When he finally opened his eyes, he saw Raven standing over him.

"Are you alright?"

"I do not know, Raven. Am I breathing?"

"You're alright. Although your arm is a mess. Let's get it wrapped so we can stop the bleeding."

Raven rummaged around the clearing until she found her satchel and pulled out her medical kit. She poured alcohol over the wounds and wrapped them in cotton bandages. She laid him next to the fire he had built and tried to revive everyone else who still lay asleep.

The green sun began to rise again, allowing them to see more clearly, although the ominous clouds still swirled above. One by one, Raven's companions awoke from the drug-induced sleep, each struggling to overcome the foggy feeling in their heads.

Raven wrapped Hadari's arm in the bandage and made a sling for him to rest his arm in to help keep it elevated. She then gave him a few swigs from a bottle of rum she had in her medical kit to help him with the pain.

When Jeffrey overcame his grogginess, he looked around and saw the creatures that Raven and Hadari had battled while the others had slept.

"What are these things?

Raven replied, "I don't know what to call them, but they were ferocious. Hadari killed most of them before I woke."

The crew spent the next hour collecting the beasts' bodies and burning them on the fire Hadari had built. The creatures smelled bad enough while alive, but their burning odor was much worse. Raven stared for a long time into the flames and found them tantalizing, almost hypnotic, as the flames danced and swirled toward the sky. After a while, she broke away from her trance.

Raven said, "Too bad we don't know much about them. They might have been able to give us a hearty meal if it hadn't been too dangerous to try it. It seems everything on this island is dangerous or poisonous."

Jeffrey asked, "Shall we continue into the forest to find what we need?"

"Yes, but I'm sending Hadari back to the ship."

Raven turned to Simba and said, "Take Hadari back to the ship and bring back twenty extra men. Make sure everyone knows how dangerous it is to touch anything. We don't want anyone else passing out on the way. We'll continue cutting a path, so you shouldn't have a problem finding your way back to us."

"Aye, Raven."

Simba collected her pistols and a machete to trek back to the beach. Hadari followed along, staying close by her. She had to hack her way through parts of the jungle where the crew had fled without being able to cut a trail. It slowed her progress, but finding their path on the return to Raven and the others would be much easier.

Raven and the rest of her crew continued past the stream, deeper into the jungle. Attila led the way, clearing a path for the others to follow. After an hour, he turned his duty over to Muzuki. Half an hour later, Muziki led them into a new clearing. The clearing wasn't grassy like the last one, nor was a stream flowing through it. Instead, it was almost desert-like. There was no plant life, only rocks, sand, and dry clay.

The clearing spread out before them, covering approximately fifty acres. As the crew walked through the area, they soon discovered holes in the ground where steam was billowing upward. As they walked past one of the openings, Raven stuck her hand out over the hole and discovered the steam was burning hot. She recoiled her hand with a little squeal.

"Be careful! The steam will burn you."

Up ahead, the group spotted one of the steam holes erupting into a water spout. The water sprayed thirty feet into the air for several seconds before returning to a column of steam. Another erupted off to their right, and another to their left.

Taylor commented, "I think these are called geysers. From what I've heard, they typically occur near volcanoes."

Raven replied, "That could be. I think that mountain up ahead is probably a volcano."

Taylor replied, "Hopefully, it doesn't plan to erupt anytime soon."

"Let's hope not."

They continued walking through the geyser field, dodging the steam columns along the way. It almost seemed the spouts were triggered whenever someone stepped near one.

Raven instructed, "Let's spread out from each other. Don't get too close, or you might set one off, burning someone else."

They tiptoed as if that might be less likely to set off one of the geysers. Every step taken seemed to release another geyser. The company of explorers constantly dodged the steam columns that sprayed into the air. Realizing that careful steps did little to ensure their safety, Raven called out to everyone, "This is getting us nowhere quickly! Let's run! Get out of here as quickly as possible!"

They trotted through the geyser field, water spouts shooting upward all around them. With every spurt of steam, another person cried out in pain. No matter how hard they tried to avoid the steam holes, another one close by turned into a spout of boiling water shooting into the air, spraying them as they ran through the field.

It seemed like a lifetime before they made it across the patch of geysers, although it only took five minutes of running. When everyone gathered at the far end of the field, they rested, gasping for air. The steam had scorched their skin, burning and blistering it. Raven passed around a small jar of ointment containing aloe to soothe their blistering skin.

Once everyone had treated their wounds, they returned to their trek through the jungle. Muziki led the way, slashing a path through the dense jungle foliage. Then, the plant life changed. Fruit trees appeared. Banana trees surrounded the group. Primates of all sorts could be seen and heard scurrying through the treetops.

Jeffrey turned around and looked at Raven, "Do we dare try to eat them?"

"What? The monkeys?"

"No, silly, the bananas."

"I'm so hungry, I'm ready to try them."

Raven reached up into one of the trees and cut down a large bunch of the fruit. She cut one of the bananas free from the bunch and peeled it to eat. The banana was not quite ripe, but Raven closed her eyes and savored its flavor. She ravenously gobbled the rest of the fruit and declared with her mouth full, "Mmm, it tastes so good!"

Everyone began grabbing the fruit from the trees, eating the bananas as if they had not eaten in weeks. The monkeys continued scurrying through the trees around them, screeching as they dove from tree to tree. The little creatures' cries intensified as the group below continued to munch on the bananas. Suddenly, all was quiet.

Raven and the others stopped in mid-chew as the jungle was no longer filled with birds singing or monkeys playing. Something was amiss. The silence filled Raven's ears.

The sound of distant thunder rumbled in her head. One short blast. Then another. Raven realized the ground beneath her feet shook with each boom of the thunder.

"What is that?" she asked no one in particular.

As they stood still, listening to the thunder, the ground shook harder and harder with each blast. They heard a mighty roar like none of them had ever heard, which blasted their eardrums. They covered their ears, trying to save their hearing. It sounded like someone blowing a trumpet; however, the noise was far more intense than any trumpet they had ever heard. The thunderous, earthshaking continued as the trumpet blasts continued and grew closer.

Raven and the others screamed with all their might but realized they couldn't hear their own screams through the thunder and trumpeting. They turned away from whatever was coming toward them and fled deeper into the jungle. Trees could be seen and heard cracking apart and crashing to the ground. The group continued to run away. No matter how fast they ran, whatever was chasing them was gaining. More trees fell to the ground behind them as they fled. A creature appeared behind them, letting out another ear-piercing trumpet as it revealed itself to the group.

CHAPTER 15

They all screamed in unison as the creature revealed itself on the path behind them. Raven had never seen such a creature before. It stood twenty-five feet tall on two legs as big as tree trunks. Two much smaller legs appeared from the creature's shoulders, like tiny little arms and hands. The creature's head seemed almost too large for its body, presenting two rows of razor-sharp teeth. Its body was covered in dark, scaly skin like a snake or a lizard. The creature saw the group and released another trumpet, signaling its intent to attack.

Everyone ran through the jungle, scattering as they went. There was no time for those at the back of the line to wait for those leading the way. The scattering seemed to confuse the creature for a moment. It looked from one tiny being to the other before choosing the closest one.

Walter was helping George as they attempted to flee. George pushed Walter away, hoping to save Walter from falling prey to the creature that had set its mind on capturing them. Walter fell over a fallen log and scrambled back to his feet, running away through the dense jungle.

George didn't bother running. He knew his time was up. He only hoped his sacrifice would allow the others to escape. The lizard-like creature took George's offering and opened its jaws as it swung its head downward, collecting George into its mouth. It bit down, crushing George's bones between its teeth amidst George's cries. The lizard raised its head into the sky and continued to chomp down on the tiny morsel of food it had found, allowing it to fall down its throat.

Raven and the others watched in horror as their companion was eaten to death by the giant lizard. Raven stood stunned at the sight of George being chewed up and swallowed by the mighty creature. Jeffrey took her by the hand and led her away, deeper into the forest.

Satisfied with its meal, the giant lizard turned and walked away, its thunderous steps fading into the jungle.

Raven and Jeffrey stopped at a stream to catch their breath after the long run from the giant lizard. Raven asked, "Was that a dragon?"

"I don't know. I have always considered dragons legendary creatures that probably never really existed."

Taylor stepped into the clearing where the two had debated the existence of dragons and said, "It wasn't a dragon. It was a dinosaur."

Raven asked, "You have seen these creatures before?"

"Not alive. I've only seen them in museums. They have been extinct for millions of years. That one, I believe, was a Tyrannosaurus rex."

Jeffrey asked, "Have you ever seen a dragon in one of your museums?"

"No, as you speculated, dragons are legendary creatures. To my knowledge, no one has ever seen a dragon or dug up one of their skeletons, as they have the Tyrannosaur."

Raven replied, "I hope you are correct. That Rexy thing..."

"Tyrannosaurus rex."

"Right. If he could fly, I would think there would be no escape."

"There were flying dinosaurs. The pterodactyl could fly."

"What did it look like?"

"They looked much like a vulture, only larger and without feathers."

Jeffrey commented, "That sounds like the creatures we saw as we sailed into this island. I thought they might be dragons, but they weren't breathing fire."

The others found their way to the stream where Raven, Jeffrey, and Taylor had settled beside them. Eight individuals gathered together to rest and quench their thirst. Taylor saw Walter walk up to the stream, but he wasn't helping George anymore.

"Where's George?"

Walter shook his head. "He didn't make it."

"What happened to him?"

"That monster ate him. Picked him up off the ground and chewed him right up."

Walter began to weep.

Taylor placed a hand on Walter's shoulder to comfort him.

"Don't worry, ole man. There was nothing you could do."

"George is the one who *could* do it. He saved me. He pushed me away and told me to run while he stayed behind and gave himself to that blasted creature."

Simba and Hadari returned to the beach, retrieved their dory, and rowed to *Destiny*. Jeremy watched from the quarterdeck as the dory approached the ship. Men and women gathered on the main deck as word got out that someone was returning.

As Simba helped Hadari climb onto the ship, Jeremy met them at the rail.

"What happened?"

Simba replied, "What didn't happen? We have been attacked by every kind of creature imaginable, and some of them you could never imagine. Ants, as big as big dogs. Dogs without hair as big as lions. Plants that shoot out poisonous darts."

"Where are Raven and the others?"

"Raven sent us back so Hadari could recover from his wounds, and I am to bring back twenty more men."

Jeremy ordered two men standing by, "Get Hadari to Mr. Greer."

"Aye, Jeremy!"

Jeremy asked, "Is Raven alright?"

"Aye. But Seremala was killed by some of the large ants."

"And Raven wants twenty more men to come to shore?"

"Aye, she needs them to help cut down trees and protect the workers as they collect timber for the rudder. It is very dangerous on this island. Everything there is potentially deadly."

John Ashworth approached the two, wearing his sword and pistols.

Jeremy asked, "Where do you think you are going, Mr. Ashworth?

"I'm going ashore to find my daughter."

"Then, who will be in charge of the ship?"

"Jeremy, my boy, you are in charge. I won't stand by and watch as you send other men ashore and leave me behind. I'm going to find Raven."

"Fine, John. I will stay behind and watch the ship while you go ashore with a new crew."

"Thank you, Jeremy."

Jeremy told one of the men, "Take the *misery whip*. You will need it to cut up the timber."

John gathered twenty men to go along with Simba onto the island. They all climbed down into the dory and rowed ashore with Simba. When they reached the shore, Simba instructed them, "The island is perilous. Be careful not to touch the vegetation, especially the flowers. Some of them shoot out poisonous darts. We will travel along a path we have already cut. Try to stay on the path. Beware of creatures like the giant ants and the hairless dogs. Everything on this island is potentially dangerous."

Simba led the way down the path. She walked, wasting no time to return to Raven and the others. She kept her sword drawn as she led the way down the path, ready for anything that might attack.

Everyone nervously followed Simba down the path through the jungle. They heard various birds chirping in the trees. Monkeys bounded from tree to tree, squawking at the intruders who had invaded their homes. Mosquitos and flies the size of large butterflies flittered in front of their faces as they walked along the path.

Simba turned and said to everyone following, "We must hurry. We should not tarry here. It is too dangerous."

She picked up the pace and led the band of explorers through the jungle. She stopped and held up her hand, signaling the others to stop, too. They listened as something significant moved through the foliage to their right. They couldn't see anything through the dense brush, only the swaying of the tall plants back and forth as something or someone pushed them aside to move through.

Simba pointed toward the movement and held her forefinger against her lips to signal everyone to remain quiet. She quietly walked down the trail, trying to avoid whatever was moving through the jungle near them. Whatever it was, it seemed to be aware that the explorers were present. The beings were moving in a direction that would eventually intersect the path Simba and the others traveled.

Simba dared not exit the path for fear that the jungle would attack with its poisonous plants or oversized insects. She led her band forward, making as little sound as possible. Simba looked into the treetops and noticed some monkeys looking downward at whatever was moving the brush along an unseen path up ahead. The monkeys were not squawking; they were only watching as whatever or whoever it was moved past the monkeys down below.

Simba increased the grip on her sword, ready for whatever might stray along her path. She stopped. She crouched low and listened. Everyone mimicked her posture and waited. Simba's leg muscles tensed. Her heart beat so fast, she thought she could hear it outside her body. Then, she realized it wasn't her heart she was hearing. Something or someone was grunting a low-pitched grunt. It wasn't just one; it was several, and they intensified.

"Ugh! Ugh! Ugh!"

They grew louder and louder as the ones making the noise came closer and closer.

"Ugh! Ugh! Ugh!"

It was coming from behind them, too.

"Ugh! Ugh! Ugh!"

Simba and the others crouched wide-eyed, searching all around as the grunts grew louder and closer. Simba raised to a battle-ready stance, and the others followed.

"Ugh! Ugh! Ugh!"

The grunts encircled them. There would be nowhere to run. Fight or surrender would be their only choice.

CHAPTER 16

John, who stood second in line, realized they were about to be attacked from all sides.

"Line formation!"

Simba faced forward toward the path yet traveled. John faced to her right. Muziki faced Simba's left. Every other man faced alternating right and left until the last man was left to cover their rear. They waited, but no attack was made.

John ordered, "Forward half-step."

Simba led them forward down the path. The grunts continued all around.

"Ugh! Ugh! Ugh!"

Their pursuers continued at their pace, never coming closer, never straying away.

Simba saw the first clearing up ahead. She pointed it out to John, who quietly passed the word down the line.

"Clearing up ahead."

Simba led them into the clearing, and the grunts continued all around them.

"Ugh! Ugh! Ugh!"

The grunts stopped once John's crew reached the center of the clearing. Simba froze. John held his fist in the air, signaling that everyone should halt.

One by one, creatures began entering the clearing. They stood upright like men, only stooped over somewhat. They each carried a weapon of sorts. Some were long pointed sticks, while others were heavier, shorter sticks like clubs. Others held a rock in their hand the size of a small cannonball.

They were covered with hair from head to toe. Each one rocked from side to side in his stance, much like John had seen chimpanzees do when they were irritated. The rocking intensified, and the creatures began another grunt in unison, only it was now a louder "Ooh! Ooh! Ooh!"

The louder their chant, the more intense their rocking. John counted as best he could. He calculated thirty of the primitive creatures against his twenty trained men.

"Circle up!"

John's men gathered into a circle facing outward to protect their backs. They spread out six feet apart to allow room to wield their weapons.

"Draw your pistols. Fire when I order. They may leave once they hear the shots."

Simba asked, "Fire into the air?"

"No, shoot to kill!"

The hairy creatures closed in one step at a time, sizing up the ability of those who had entered their domain. Still swaying as they approached. Still singing at their enemy. "Ooh! Ooh! Ooh!"

When they came within ten yards of their enemy, John ordered, "Ready pistols!"

Everyone raised and cocked their weapons and waited. The creatures continued forward, now jumping and waving their weapons at the intruders, trying to intimidate them if possible.

"Fire!"

Twenty shots rang out, filling the air with smoke and the smell of sulfur. "Ooos" turned into cries of fright, pain, and shock. When the air cleared, John's crew saw twelve of the creatures lying on the ground, dead or near death. Eighteen more were running for the jungle and their lives.

John and the others approached the bodies lying on the ground. He rolled the first body over with his foot to examine its face. John was puzzled by the creature that lay at his feet. It looked like a man, but there was far too much hair. Its forehead was sloped more like an ape's than a man's. Its eyes were sunken into its brow. Its mouth protruded from its face, and its teeth stuck out like a dog's muzzle.

Simba turned to John and asked, "Have you ever seen anything like this before?"

"Aye. Once, long ago. I was a boy traveling to Bristol to get away from those who would force me into servitude. A menagerie was traveling on the same road I was. They invited me to join them, but I declined. One of the people who traveled with them looked like this. They called him a werewolf. Half man, half wolf."

"There is such a creature as this, werewolf?"

"I don't know. There are legends about people who turn into wolves when the moon is full. They kill and feed on other humans. Ghost stories, if you ask me."

Simba asked, "Then what do you think these creatures are?"

"I have no idea, but I think we need to find Raven before we come in contact with any more."

Raven and the others continued walking along a stream that seemed to be flowing away from the mountain. Attila continued cutting a path as they traveled deeper and deeper into the island. The vegetation began to change. Raven could see Mahogany trees standing straight and strong just up ahead. Her countenance lifted as she realized they were nearing the end of their search for the much-needed timber. They began to walk faster, sensing that they were close.

Finally, they reached a part of the forest filled with the tall, dark-wooded trees they had desired. Raven picked out a tree with a diameter base of at least three feet.

"This will be perfect for our rudder."

Mdago and Mtamu approached the large tree with their axes and began swinging them at the giant tree. Although Mtamu was a woman, she was powerful and capable of wielding her axe. With each swing, the chops echoed throughout the forest. Chips of wood flew away from the tree's base with each strike of their axes. Raven and the others watched as the two rhythmically swung their blades against the tree's trunk.

After a while, Mvuvi and Bila Meno took over, swinging the axes.

"Whack, whack! Whack, whack!"

The men continued swinging their axes with little success. After an hour of chopping, they had barely cut an eight-inch notch in the side of the tree. The axes were turned back into the hands of Mdago and Mtamu, but before they continued their chopping, they took time to sharpen the edges of the axe blades. By the time the blades were sharp enough to continue, night fell, and Raven called for everyone to settle in for the night.

Muziki and Attila worked together to build a fire to help keep away any unwanted creatures during the night. Everyone took out their satchels and found something they could eat. Taylor and Walter had no supplies, so several men shared food with the two.

Raven slept very little during the night. She was too nervous about the creatures that might be lurking in the jungle around them. Her mind raced as she thought about all the beings they had encountered in the jungle so far. She listened to the insects chirping in the breezy night air. She heard Jeffrey breathing, gasping as he slept without a care. Raven rolled over closer to him, resting her back against his to receive some of his warmth. After a moment, Jeffrey stirred, rolled over to face Raven's back, and wrapped his arm around her to give her even more warmth. Finally, Raven fell asleep.

Early the following day, they all woke to the rumbling from the nearby mountain. The ground shook under their feet, giving them the sense that it was shifting beneath them. Raven felt that, at one point, the ground might open up and swallow them.

"We have to get the tree down and quickly!"

The men took turns swinging the axes against the giant Mahogany. They struck the tree as fast as they could. Once a man's energy was spent, he passed the axe to the next. Even Charles Taylor and Walter took their turn at swinging an axe.

Finally, the tree began to sway in the wind. Raven watched as the giant tree tilted its top toward the mountain.

"It's ready to fall! Be careful!"

As the tree began to fall, loud cracks were heard as it split apart and broke away from its base. Everyone scattered, looking upward to see which way the tree would fall. They stepped far enough away from the tree in case it happened to swing in an unexpected direction. The cracking continued as the tree fell in slow motion. It fell to the earth with a loud crash, its base bouncing once off the ground until resting on the surface.

Out of nowhere, Simba arrived with John and his crew into the clearing where the giant tree lay. Raven smiled as she saw her papa was among them. She walked to him.

"What are you doing here, Papa?"

"Well, I wasn't going to let you have all the fun. Besides, I missed you."

Raven hugged him and said to everyone, "Let's finish this job and be on our way.

The first thing they did was even off the end of the tree where it had been chopped. Two men grabbed the whipsaw, affectionately called the misery whip, and began sawing the end of the tree. After a while, two more men took over the sawing duties. The tree proved to be just as challenging to cut through as it was to chop with the axe. After several pairs of men had taken a turn at the misery whip, the tree's base fell away.

Raven stepped off twelve feet down the length of the fallen tree to mark where they should make the next cut. Then, the sawing commenced. Pairs of men took turns using the misery whip to cut through the unwilling tree.

Something fell from the sky and hit Raven on the top of the shoulder. She started to brush it away and realized what it was as she did.

"Ugh! It's dung!"

Raven brushed away the dung and looked up to see where it had come from. Twenty feet above her sat a strange-looking ape-like creature with long reddish hair. The ape was fat and looked unconcerned. He had a huge pouch of flesh and blubber under his chin.

Taylor saw the creature, "That looks like an orangutan."

Raven asked, "An orangutan?"

"Yes. They live primarily in Borneo. I saw some once in a zoo in Chicago. They can be quite mischievous, and they are highly intelligent."

Raven replied, "And apparently quite a good aim when it comes to disposing of their dung. Captain Billings has much better manners when it comes to relieving himself."

"Captain Billings?"

"Yes. My monkey. I raised him from a baby. I found him on an island about four years ago. He had been either abandoned or his mother had died, so I took care of him."

Turner replied, "Oh, I can't wait to meet him."

At mid-afternoon, they managed to finish the cross-cut of the log, and it fell to the ground with a thud. Now, it was time to start splitting the log apart to make long, wide planks to be used on the rudder. They hammered several heavy metal wedges into the log as it rested on the ground. Since there had been no lower branches, they hoped it would split evenly, giving them nice straight boards for the rudder. Still, the wood was quite hard, and getting the wedges to penetrate the log's surface was difficult. It was like trying to drive a nail into a stone. But with persistence, they got the wedges driven into the log and managed to split away a section, leaving the log with a relatively flat surface on one side.

They started another split line down the length of the log, about two inches from the edge they had just split. This would give them their first plank. They hammered the wedges into the log, and after an hour or so, a nice two-inch board split away from the log.

They continued splitting boards away from the log while others of the crew used drawing knives to smooth out the surfaces of each plank. By nightfall, they had two complete boards ready to be carried back to the ship.

Chapter 17

The men were exhausted after a long day of swinging axes, whipping cross-cut saws, and smoothing out the boards with drawing knives. They caught some fish swimming in the nearby stream and roasted them over the fire for supper. After eating their fill of the fish and some bananas they found nearby, they collapsed into a deep sleep. Two men John had brought from the ship, Juniper and Haggard, stood the first watch.

The night air was once again cold and breezy as everyone else bedded down. Raven took her spot next to Jeffrey, and they lay close to each other to receive warmth. The mountain glowed a bright orange, fiery color that illuminated the camp. The bowels of the mountain rumbled and roared throughout the night. Occasionally, the ground shook, reminding everyone they should be wary of the mountain's imminent danger.

After four hours, Simba and Bila Meno relieved Juniper and Haggard from the watch. All seemed quiet at first, but after an hour or so, the sounds of the night went silent. No longer could Simba hear the insects chirping in the darkness—no more chattering of the monkeys or other creatures that lived in the trees above. Even the mountain seemed to quiet its rumbling. Simba felt something was nearing the camp. Some danger was afoot. She crept over to where Raven was sleeping and nudged her captain to wake her.

Raven roused and looked up at the tall, slender warrior woman.

"What is it?" she whispered.

"I'm not sure, but something is wrong. Listen."

Raven sat still and said, "I hear nothing."

"Exactly. Where are the birds, the insects, the monkeys? It is too quiet."

Raven nudged Jeffrey to wake him and put a finger to her lips to quiet him.

"What is it?"

"I don't know. Quietly wake the others."

Jeffrey moved about the camp, walking softly from man to man. He woke each one and told them to stay alert and remain quiet. Raven and Simba stood together, searching the darkness for signs of danger.

Raven heard a rustle in the trees near where Bila Meno was standing watch. Raven used her hand to shield the firelight from her eyes so she could see better in the darkness. Bila Meno was not there.

Raven asked Simba, "Where's Bila?"

Simba shielded her eyes just as Raven had and searched the darkness for her watch partner.

"I don't know," she whispered. "He was just there."

Raven and Simba crept to where Bila Meno had been standing watch and searched for him. Raven's foot stumbled over something on the ground. She knelt to inspect it and found a pistol lying before her. Raven looked back at Simba as she raised the pistol for Simba to see.

"Bring a light."

Simba crept back to the fire and brought back a burning stick for Raven to use as a torch. Raven waved the torch along the ground's surface, looking for footprints. She found a disturbance in the dust where several feet had shuffled around. One set of prints wore boots, while the other set seemed to be unshod.

Raven raised her torch toward the jungle and listened for any movement. She heard nothing. She saw nothing. Slowly, one by one, the sounds of the jungle returned. The insects were chirping. The birds began singing their early morning songs. The green sunlight began to illuminate the sky once more. The morning had dawned, and Raven felt anxious for her man, Bila Meno.

"Strike camp! Attila, stay here with ten men and finish the work on the lumber. The rest of you, arm yourselves and prepare to move out. We have a man missing."

John led the way through the jungle, following the tracks. Since a compass was useless on the island, there was no way to tell in what direction the tracks were following. As best they could tell, they were moving along the mountain's base in a counterclockwise direction.

They traveled through a grove of banana trees and began picking the fruit as they walked along. They munched on the bananas as they followed John's path. Up ahead, Raven noticed some familiar-looking flowers.

"Papa, be careful of those flowers. They're poisonous. They shoot out little darts that will put you to sleep."

John raised his eyebrows in disbelief but continued down the path. He unsheathed his sword and touched one of the blooms with the blade. Immediately, a pestle shot out and embedded in the trunk of a nearby tree. John looked back at Raven with amazement as she said, "I told you so."

John walked through the area where the dangerous flowers grew, keeping his distance as best he could. Since he was the largest man on the crew by far, he would need to be more careful than the others as he walked along the path. Large bees the size of the cockroaches they had all seen at Port St. Felix buzzed around the center of the giant flowers. John winced, thinking the bees might set off the dangerous darts of the blossoms. For some reason, the bees didn't seem to affect the triggering mechanism of the poisonous darts.

Eventually, they came to a clearing. In the open field, they spotted a group of large animals the size of elephants, maybe larger.

Raven commented, "Those look like a rhinoceros except for that plate at the back of their heads, and they're much larger, of course."

Taylor replied, "Those are Triceratops. Another kind of dinosaur."

"What should we do?"

"Don't worry. They aren't meat eaters. They graze on plant life. We should be alright if we don't disturb them."

They continued to move through the clearing, tiptoeing and swinging widely to avoid the gigantic creatures. John pointed out a mound off to their right. It didn't take long for them to realize what it was. The smell was unbearable. A dung pile lay ten feet away. It stood five feet tall and was swarmed by flies the size of an average man's fist.

Raven asked Taylor, "Ugh, do they all relieve themselves in the same spot like that?"

"No, I think that is just one trip to the privy."

"You've got to be joking!"

"No. I'm not joking. If one lifts his tail, you don't want to stand near him."

One of the large creatures lifted his tail to their right as if on cue.

With her nose wrinkled, Raven said, "Kind of reminds me of what Mr. Gant used to deposit in his chamber pot."

John turned and chuckled his deep, billowing laugh at Raven's comment.

Several minutes later, they reached the opposite edge of the clearing. They lost the tracks they had been following because they detoured to avoid the dinosaurs.

"We need to spread out and look for their tracks. Fire a shot into the air if you find anything."

The band split into groups and followed different trajectories through-out the clearing. Raven, John, and Jeffrey circled around to the right, while Taylor, Walter, and some of the others circled to the left. The field they searched must have been at least forty acres. The direction Raven took led them back to where the dinosaurs were grazing. In the distance, Raven and her crew watched two of the large creatures sparring with one another. The two were not as large as some they had seen. Raven decided they must be juveniles doing what juveniles do: jousting and developing their fighting skills. Even though it seemed only to be play, the crash of the two knocking heads was thunderous.

Raven led them, taking a wide path around the giant creatures, trying to avoid them. One of the adult dinosaurs took notice of the tiny creatures scurrying past her while she munched on the tall vegetation growing along the edge of the jungle. Raven was nervous as they trotted along, looking for tracks of the beings who had stolen Bila Meno.

Suddenly, the juvenile dinosaurs stopped their jousting. The adults raised their heads, listening. The babies gathered with their mothers. Something was amiss. The ground began to shake. Raven and the others stopped and listened. A thunderous roar pierced the wind. The dinosaurs retreated into the open field, running away from the jungle. Raven looked toward the jungle and witnessed large trees being knocked to the ground as something moved toward the clearing. Whatever it was, it was moving right toward her and her men.

"Run!"

They fled along the edge of the clearing, trying to avoid whatever was moving toward them. Another roar pierced their ears. Raven glanced over her right shoulder in time to see another of the giant lizard-like crea-tures that had captured and eaten George. It roared again as it parted the trees and entered the clearing on two legs. Everyone followed Raven as she ducked into the jungle to hide from the monster. They turned and watched the creature as it pursued the rhino-like dinosaurs through the clearing.

Then, two of the four-legged rhinodinos turned on the pursuer to protect their young. One of them rammed into the larger dinosaur, knocking it to the ground backward. The other rhinosaur took advantage of the opportunity and lunged its pointed nose-horn into the side of the fallen lizard. It backed up to ascertain the damage it had inflicted. The rexysaur stumbled to its feet, bleeding from its side. It limped back toward the jungle as its two attackers pursued, nudging him with the tip of their horns. Satisfied that the rexy would not return, they turned to one another and roared before returning to their herd.

Raven and her crew continued to look for tracks along the edge of the clearing. It wasn't long before John noticed a notch on the jungle's edge. In the notch were several pairs of footprints.

"I think I found them."

Raven walked over to inspect the tracks.

"Yes, I think you're right. These look like the same tracks we saw back at our camp."

Raven pulled out her pistol and fired into the air. Birds, frightened by the unfamiliar sound of gunfire, leaped into the air and flew deeper into the jungle. A moment later, another shot was fired in the distance. Simba and the others had heard Raven's shot and would soon join them where they stood. Ten minutes later, John spotted the other crew trotting across the field to join them at the edge of the clearing.

When they arrived, Simba panted, "You found… the tracks?"

Raven replied, "We did. After you catch your breath, we'll continue."

"I'm alright. Let's go. Bila has already been gone too long."

"Are you sure?"

Simba nodded, bent her head down, and motioned toward the jungle, indicating they should move out. John continued to lead the way while Simba and her crew brought up the rear.

The vegetation was not as dense here as it was where they followed the tracks. However, daylight was leaving, and it was more challenging to see the footprints. Within an hour, the sun's green light had faded into black, and they had no choice but to slow their pace. They dare not stop. Bila Meno had been gone for almost a day. There was nowhere to camp without exposing themselves to the ones who had captured Bila.

They continued to follow John through the darkness. An echo of rumbles bled through the trees toward them—faintly at first, but the sound grew in intensity as they continued forward.

Then, they recognized it.

"Ugh! Ugh! Ugh!"

It was the same chant they had heard before.

"Ugh! Ugh! Ugh!"

They crept closer, trying to remain invisible to those they had pursued.

"Ugh! Ugh! Ugh!"

The chants grew louder and louder and.... stopped.

CHAPTER 18

Raven and her crew crept through the jungle toward the area where they had heard the grunts. All seemed quiet. No insects were chirping, and no birds were singing. The only sound they heard was their footsteps crunching along the sandy path.

They heard a man scream. They all froze as their blood chilled their bones. They heard more grunts and mumbling up ahead. John led the way as they burst into a small clearing at the mountain's base. Several of the hairy men-like creatures they had dealt with before were gathered in front of a cave. They encircled something lying on the ground and grabbed and pulled it apart. They grunted and snarled as they began to eat the flesh of some animal. There was no fire; they were eating it raw. They had no knives to cut away the flesh from the bone; they pulled the flesh away with their teeth. Some of them opened up the animal's torso with their claw-like fingers, pulled out its entrails, and ate them too. Raven and the others were disgusted by the sight.

They crept closer, searching for Bila Meno, hoping he might still be alive. Maybe he was being held captive inside the cave. Raven decided they would confront the creatures. She motioned for her men to spread out in a semicircle around the cave where the creatures were eating. They carefully approached the cave, where the feasters were still ripping meat away from the bone.

As they ate, Raven noticed something lying on the ground at the creatures' feet. Shoes, rags, a belt, and a pistol lay on the ground. Raven realized she was witnessing the consumption of one of her crew—Bila Meno. She was horrified at the realization that one of her men was being eaten by such savage creatures. Her horror soon turned to grief, then anger, and then rage.

Raven drew her sword and marched toward the creatures. She said nothing. She didn't scream. With tears in her eyes, she swung her cutlass over and over, slashing the hairy creatures. Some of them tried to flee, but Raven's men were ready. They attacked with pistols and swords, cutting each of the creatures down. They hacked off their arms. They cut them off at their knees. They separated the heads from the bodies.

More creatures came running from within the cave with sticks in hand, running toward their attackers. Even though they outnumbered Raven's men, they were no match against swords, knives, and pistols.

No one but Raven knew why they were attacking the creatures as they came bounding from the cave, but attack they did. John drove his sword into the belly of one of the man-apes. Jeffrey fired his pistol at one of the attackers, shooting him in the face. The creature fell backward and died, his face splattered with blood and brains. John plunged his long knife into the throat of one and swung his cutlass, clearing another one's head from its body. On and on, they fought as more of the creatures exited the cave and ran toward them. But in only minutes, the creatures were eliminated.

Raven stood panting. Her chest heaved while her eyes were wide with anger. John walked over to his daughter and touched her shoulder.

Raven growled and raised her cutlass to attack him. John blocked her sword with his own.

"Raven!"

She froze. She stared at her papa, rage still in her eyes.

"Raven. It's me. Your papa."

Reality began to return to her. Her face relaxed. She dropped her cutlass and stood weeping. John wrapped her in his arms. Raven sobbed into her papa's bosom.

John and the others still didn't understand what had upset their captain. As he looked around the area to assess the damage, he was horrified to find a head lying on the ground. It was Bila Meno. His head had been ripped from his body. He had been disemboweled, and his limbs had been ripped away and partially eaten.

"Now I know what is wrong with Raven. These creatures have killed and eaten our friend Bila Meno."

The others were shocked by John's words. Jeffrey walked to Raven and touched her shoulder while she stood in her father's embrace.

"Raven, I'm so sorry. What a horrible thing to witness."

Raven freed herself from her father, turned to Jeffrey, and fell into his arms as she continued to cry. Jeffrey said nothing else; he just stood there, holding onto her.

Raven had lost another of her crew to the brutal cruelty of the island. Another of her trusted crew had been killed while under her command. When would it end? How many more must die? Yes, they had chosen to follow her, but did they realize how dangerous it would be? She struggled with her thoughts as she wept against Jeffrey's shoulder.

John interrupted her self-loathing when he said, "We should burn Bila's body so that no other creatures will feed on him."

John and the others gathered wood to build a large fire to cremate Bila Meno's body. They gathered the pieces of his body and placed them on the woodpile before igniting the fire. They stood by and watched as the blaze consumed the body of their friend. Flames reached up twenty feet into the air. The fire sizzled as the fat and meat of the body burned. Sparks floated into the sky like Bila's soul was traveling away from Earth and into heaven. Everyone stood and watched, saying their goodbyes to their fallen friend. Finally, John interrupted everyone's thoughts.

"We should go back to Attila and the others. There is still much to do."

One by one, they left the fire as it continued to burn. They walked back to where they had left Attila. The walk back was very solemn for them all. No one said a word as they passed through the jungle.

Butterflies the size of hawks fluttered past them as they walked along the trail. Reds, yellows, and blues bounced through the air as the crew returned to the rest of their people. As she strolled down the path, a yellow and black butterfly landed on Raven's shoulder. She looked to her shoulder without turning her head. She became amused and delighted by the sizeable winged insect as it rested upon her. Her mood lightened a little, and she grinned. The butterfly hummed in Raven's ear as it flapped its wings back and forth. Raven realized she had never heard a butterfly before. They were so small compared to this one, and she guessed their sounds were so minute they couldn't be heard by the human ear. Then, the insect fluttered off her shoulder back into the air and flew away.

Raven still mourned her friend as she walked along the path, but she thought somehow Bila Meno had spoken to her through the butterfly. It was as if his spirit had left his body and entered the butterfly, telling her he was all right. His body was gone, but his spirit was still alive, now living in the butterfly's body. She smiled.

They continued down the path leading back to where Attila and the others were working on the new rudder. The jungle seemed more alive today. The birds' songs were almost deafening. Black apes with long, spindly arms hooted and howled as they swung through the trees.

In the distance, they could hear the faint chops of axes being swung against hardwood. Raven felt relief that they were nearing their return to the others. They reached the clearing where the rhinosaurs had been before, but this time, the area was clear of the large leathery creatures. Raven and the others scattered about since no path was needed to comply with.

The green sun burned hot against their bare skin as they traipsed through the clearing. Raven began to sweat beneath her leather garments. The heat was taking its toll on the travelers who were no longer protected by the jungle canopy. Raven longed to be back on the ocean where she could bathe in the coolness of the winds as they pushed her ship along the waters. She realized she was parched. Her lips were cracking. Her tongue felt dry like a cotton ball. Raven felt lightheaded as her strength faded. Her steps became labored. She stumbled along the dry ground that had been scorched by the sun.

Raven stopped.

"Quiet!"

The others stopped, too.

"Listen."

They heard a faint rumble in the distance behind them. They turned to search the edge of the clearing from where they had traveled. The rumbling increased. Raven noticed a slight movement among the trees in the jungle at the mountain's base. Something was parting the trees, creating a path for itself. The jungle creatures were now silent. No birds sang, no apes howled.

Suddenly, everything erupted as flocks of birds swarmed into the clearing as they fled their homes in the jungle. The birds screeched and chirped in fear as they flew toward Raven and her band. Other animals entered the clearing on foot. Herds of wild pigs, deer, antelope, and buffalo stampeded the area, scattering in all directions.

Out of the jungle appeared one of the rexysaurs. Raven thought all the animals were running from it. It wasn't true. The rexysaur was fleeing as well. The twenty-acre clearing was now filled with every imaginable creature there was. All of them are fleeing something even more deadly than any of them.

An earth-shaking roar escaped the jungle. It shook the ground like an earthquake. And then, a creature more significant and hideous than any they had seen yet stepped into the clearing. It was twice the size of the rexysaur, standing nearly sixty feet high. The monster roared again, presenting several rows of razor-sharp teeth. It typically walked on all four of its legs but would sometimes stand upright on its back legs to roar at any creature who was near enough to see it. When it dropped back down to its four-legged position, the earth shook. The creature appeared to move in slow motion, but it could easily catch up to any fleeing animal because it was so large.

Raven watched as the mega-sized dinosaur reached forward with one of its front feet, with long, sharp talons on the tips of its digits. He scooped up a handful of beasts on the clearing floor and shoveled them into his mouth. He raised his head toward the sky as he chomped on the meaty morsels, trying to keep them from falling out of his mouth.

The herds of wild game were nearing Raven and the others. They had to turn and run into the jungle to escape the stampede. They could no longer be concerned about staying on the path. They each made a new path as they ran through the jungle blindly. Eventually, they all became separated and ran as best they could in what they hoped would be the right direction.

Raven saw several deer running at her. She dove to the ground and waited as the deer hurdled over her and disappeared into the jungle. In the distance, Raven heard a familiar yell.

"Raven!"

"Jeffrey!?"

"Raven! Come quickly!"

Raven thought the cries were coming from her right. She ran as best she could toward the yells, but the foliage was too thick. She removed her sword and used it like a machete to clear a path. The call was slowing and somewhat muffled as it continued.

"Raven! Hurry!"

"I'm coming, Jeffrey!"

Chapter 19

Raven began to cry, with tears running down her face as she feared she might not find him in time. *What was happening to him?*

"Jeffrey, I'm coming!"

The trees opened up to a small clearing. Raven froze as she saw Jeffrey's head and one of his arms sticking out of the ground. The rest of him had disappeared. Raven rushed forward, but Jeffrey stopped her.

"Don't! Stay right there!"

Raven started to step forward anyway, but her foot sank into the sand. She recoiled her foot and realized what it was. She had heard of it but had never seen it before. *Quicksand!*

"It's no use, Raven. Stay away. The more I struggle, the quicker I sink."

"Jeffrey, hang on! Please! I'll get you out!"

"I love you, Raven. I always have."

"Don't worry, I'll find something to drag you out with."

Raven turned back to the jungle to search for anything that would help. She found a vine hanging from a tree and yanked on its end, trying to free it. She had freed enough, she thought, to reach Jeffrey and pull him out. She hacked at the vine with her sword, gathered it up, and ran back to where she had left Jeffrey.

When she arrived, all that was left of him were the tips of his fingers sticking out of the sand. She threw one end of the vine at the protruding hand and hoped he could grab it.

"Jeffrey! Reach out and grab the vine!"

His finger didn't move. The vine lay against his fingers, but his fingers didn't move. They disappeared into the sand. Jeffrey was gone.

Raven wailed as she realized he was gone. Over and over, she called his name and cried, "Jeffrey! Jeffery! Don't go! You can't give up!"

She thought if she tied the vine around the base of a tree and around her waist, maybe she could reach down and find him. John suddenly appeared from the jungle with a puzzled look.

"Raven? What's wrong?"

"Oh, Papa! Jeffrey fell into this quicksand, and I need to get him out."

"How long has he been under?"

"I don't know. I went to get this vine so I could pull him out. When I got back, only his hand was sticking out. Then, it went under, too. Please, Papa, we have to get him out."

"I'm sorry, Raven. You won't be able to reach him. Even if you could, he's likely already dead."

Raven continued to cry and wail over Jeffrey's disappearance. She could bear no more loss. It seemed she was losing everyone in her life whom she cared about. She couldn't lose another, especially Jeffery.

The others eventually gathered together at the quicksand once they heard Raven's wails. Raven wept into her papa's chest as they all arrived. The Megasaur's roar filled the air all around them. It was still on the hunt and was coming closer.

John commanded, "We have to get out of here. Everyone, run that way!"

They all turned away from the quicksand, ran back into the jungle, and away from the Megasaur's growls. John had to drag Raven away and into the jungle while she still sobbed. Simba led the way as they all ran away from the giant creatures, yelling. After a mile of running, they all fell exhausted to the ground, sure that the dinosaur was no longer following them.

Simba strolled to Raven and sat beside her while Raven continued to sob.

"Raven, I know this is very difficult for you. We have all lost someone. Mothers, fathers, brothers, sisters, and lovers. You need to compose yourself. Your men depend on you."

"They shouldn't. I am a terrible leader. All I've done is lead them to death. How many more will die because of my poor decisions?"

"None of this is your fault. You have no control over what life presents to us. Some of us will die. You can't control when or how it happens, no more than you can change the stars in the sky. If you think you can, then you think too highly of yourself."

"But, I led them here."

"No! We were brought here by a higher power. You had no control over it. You did not cause the storm to bring us here or to damage our ship. You had no way of knowing that this island would be so strange and so dangerous. Raven, you have lost your way. Much has happened to your crew over the past year. You have lost many men and women, but it was not your fault. You are a good leader. If you were not, we would not follow you. You must understand that we love and admire you, all of us. And we will follow you to the end. But, we need you to be who you were, the Red Raven, not some silly little girl who shakes with fear at the slightest sign of danger."

Raven stared into Simba's eyes, realizing the young woman was right. Raven had somehow lost her confidence. She had lost her mettle. How could she lead her crew without them? She sniffed and wiped away her tears, took a deep breath, and resolved never to succumb to self-doubt again. Yes, she had lost Jeffrey, the one she loved the most besides her papa. But she couldn't succumb to self-loathing, doubt, and fear.

"You're right, Simba. I have allowed myself to become weak. It won't happen again."

Raven gathered her crew together to show she could still lead.

"I apologize for the way that I've acted of late. I want you to know it won't happen again. We still have much to do, so let's get moving and find our way back to Attila and the others."

Everyone felt a bit refreshed, seeing their captain had regained her composure. Their moods lightened a bit; however, they were still aware of the dangers of the island's jungle. Since they had been scattered about, returning to Attila proved to be more complicated than they would have hoped. There was no path they could follow, and the sun was not a dependable means to guide their direction. Raven decided they would walk together in pairs, spreading about thirty feet apart to stay within shouting distance. If someone happened upon the trail they had cut earlier, they would call the rest of the crew to join them. If someone happened upon danger, they could call for help.

They trekked through the jungle, searching for the trail that would lead them back to Attila and his crew, who were working on constructing a new rudder. Raven thought they should be able to hear the sound of metal against wood as the men worked on the rudder. There should have been the sound of chopping or scraping the drawing knife against the wood's edge as they shaped it into planks. But all was relatively quiet up ahead. Raven began to doubt that they were going in the right direction. Without a compass or the sun's dependability to point them in a direction, it wasn't easy to tell whether they were traveling in a straight line. For all she knew, they were walking in circles.

The green sun began to lower itself behind the fiery mountain. Raven decided she needed to call everyone together to camp for the night. As each group returned to Raven's position, she noticed who returned. There should have been a total of twenty in their camp, including Charles Taylor and his companion, Walter. Two were missing.

"Who is missing?" asked Raven.

Everyone looked around, trying to figure out who had not returned to camp.

"Where is Kifaru?"

"I am here, Raven."

Raven tried to recall who should be there. She glanced around and saw Taylor and Walter, John and Simba, Kifaru and Mtamu.

"Where is Mdago?"

Everyone looked around. He had not yet arrived.

"Who was Mdago traveling with?"

Simba replied, "Mdago and Muziki were together."

Raven asked, "Who was closest to Mdago and Muziki?"

Mvuvi replied, "Kifaru and I were closest to them. They were on the far left of us. They were still there when we heard the call to return to you. They heard the call, too. They acknowledged that they were right behind us. But I haven't seen them since."

Raven thought, "*Wonderful! Our crew is growing smaller and smaller.*"

"Well, we can't look for them now. It's too dark and too dangerous. Let's build a fire and bed down for the night. We'll look for them tomorrow."

Muziki and Mdago heard Kifaru call out, "Raven is calling us back to make camp for the night."

Muziki replied, "Alright. We are coming."

As the two began tracing their way back toward Kifaru, Muziki stopped. "Look! This looks like the trail we have been looking for."

Muziki examined the spot more carefully, turning one way then another. "Yes, this is the trail."

Mdago said, "Hurry! We must tell Raven we have found the trail."

They looked up to find Kifaru, but he had already left. They looked to their right and then to their left. He was nowhere to be found. They looked for the mountain to see which direction they should look in, but the mountain was no longer visible. The sun had fallen to the ground behind the mountain, and they could not tell which direction they had been walking toward or where they had come from. They were lost in the dark.

Muziki called out, "Kifaru! Kifaru! Where are you?"

No one answered. They stood motionless, hoping to hear their friends in the distance. Looking for a sign of which direction they should travel. They waited in total darkness. Muziki's knees began to shake. His lower lip began to quiver. He could barely make out the silhouette of his companion standing next to him.

Mdago whispered to his friend, "I do not like this."

"I don't either, but we can not move. It is too dark for us to try to find our way back to Raven."

They stood together, holding onto one another, shaking with fear. Suddenly, something moved in the distance, something moving through the brush. Whatever it was, it was moving slowly through the jungle and toward them.

"What is that, Muziki?"

"I don't know," he whispered. "But keep your voice low."

They stood face to face, holding onto each other. They looked in the same direction as they continued to hear something moving in the distance. A pair of orange eyes peered at them through the foliage. The eyes held still, watching them. Although Muziki and Mdago could not see the creature in the darkness, they were confident it could see them. The eyes never blinked and never moved. They only stared at the pair, who were shuddering in fear. The creature could smell their fear. Its senses heightened with the realization that its next meal was very close.

Muziki whispered, "Mdago, do not run. Back away slowly. Do not turn your back on it, or it will surely attack."

Mdago's voice quivered, "Alright. I will not run."

They backed away from the eyes, glancing backward to avoid stumbling but never turning their backs on the creature. Muziki edged away from his companion, leaving the eyes to decide which of them it would pursue.

Mdago whispered, "Where are you going?"

"Keep going. I will try to lead it away from you. Find a place to hide."

Mdago whimpered as he continued to step backward into the jungle. He backed himself up against a large tree. The tree had a branch hanging down low enough that Mdago could reach it. He jumped, grasped the limb, and pulled himself up, leaving the ground. As he did, he heard an intense growl right below him. It sounded like a lion, but he still couldn't see the creature.

He climbed the tree higher and higher as he heard the animal try to swat him out of the tree. The creature managed to lift itself onto the first branch and began climbing toward Mdago. Mdago climbed high through the tree, but the creature closed in on him. He decided to climb out onto one of the branches that reached out to the next tree. He hoped he could move to another tree to escape the animal. Mdago leaped but fell eight feet before gripping a limb from another tree. It was a much smaller tree, but Mdago managed to stop his fall as he held onto one of the small branches.

Mdago looked above him to see the creature jumping toward the tree he had just entered. A dim light from the moon illuminated the creature enough that Mdago could see it was indeed a lion. But not just a lion. It was the most enormous lion he had ever seen, with long, sharp fangs hanging out of its mouth like tusks on an elephant. It roared as it landed in Mdago's tree and began slipping down to him. Mdago shimmied down, but he wasn't fast enough. He gave up, let go of the tree, and allowed himself to fall to the ground. He landed with a thud, and he lost his breath. He gasped for air, but it seemed it would never return. Finally, he regained his breath, but it was too late to regain his composure. The lion landed on Mdago with the full force of her weight, crushing Mdago beneath her. Mdago wasn't quite dead when the lioness began to eat him. He screamed as the lion tore his flesh away from his bones. Over and over, the lioness bit into his flesh as he screamed until he lost consciousness and felt the relief of death.

Chapter 20

The next morning, as the green sun began to rise, Raven roused everyone, anxious to find her missing men.

"Get up, everyone. We need to find Mdago and Muziki."

They all did as Raven ordered, collecting their things and packing them up so they could begin the search for the missing men. Raven led the way as they headed through the jungle toward the area where Muziki and Mdago had last been heard. They followed a path made by her men returning to her last night. Raven counted off ten yards in her mind as she traveled along the path. Each group of men was set thirty feet apart as they searched the jungle. If she measured where each group had traveled, she hoped she could find the last place her missing men were heard to be.

Once they reached the thirty-foot mark, they slowed their pace, and Raven asked that everyone spread out and search for any sign of the missing men. After a short period of searching, Raven led them down the path for another thirty feet, where they searched again.

An hour passed as they searched. Raven led them down the fourth leg of the trail, searching for any sign of Mdago or Muziki. Up ahead, Raven saw a body lying just off the path. She ran up to see who it was.

"Muziki! Muziki, are you alright?"

She shook the man, trying to wake him.

"Raven? Is that you?"

"Muziki, where is Mdago?"

"We got separated. An enormous lion was stalking us. We tried to get back to you, but Mdago lagged behind, and I heard him scream several times. The lion must have gotten him."

"I'm glad you're alright, Muziki. We'll search some more to see if we can find Mdago."

"Oh, Raven, I found the trail we were looking for. It is just up ahead."

"Fine. You can show me as we search for Mdago."

They continued down the path, searching for their missing friend. Less than thirty feet away, Muziki pointed out, "Raven, this is the trail we were looking for, is it not?"

"Yes, I believe you're right. We'll continue looking for Mdago, then return to this trail."

Raven led the way down the path as they searched for any sign of Mdago. Fifty feet later, she found a spot where the brush was disturbed. A large tree with low-hanging branches had gashes in its bark around the trunk, beginning about twelve feet from the ground. Raven looked up to see if there was any sign of Mdago. She saw broken branches about halfway up the tree. She could almost make out a trail through the branches where something huge had forced its way through the limbs. Claw marks were spread from branch to branch, leading to the next tree.

Raven walked over to examine the tree next to it. It was a smaller tree, much smaller than the first. Around the base of the smaller tree, Raven found what looked like dried blood. She circled the tree and noticed drag marks on the ground. Two small trenches lead away from the tree into the jungle. In the midst of one of the trenches was a leather shoe. Raven recognized it as a shoe one of her crew had worn whenever they left the ship to travel on dry ground. Raven picked up the shoe and saw it was covered in blood. She gasped. Inside the shoe was a foot that had been severed from its leg. Raven dropped the shoe as tears formed in her eyes.

Simba asked, "What is it?"

Simba picked up the shoe to see what Raven had seen. She was disgusted by the sight of the severed foot still resting in the shoe. Simba turned to the others and said, "It is Mdago's foot."

John stepped forward to comfort his daughter, but she raised her hand and said, "I'm alright."

She took only a moment to compose herself before she said, "Mdago is gone. There is nothing we can do for him. Let's get back to the trail."

Raven brushed past her crew and led the way back to the trail that Muziki had pointed out to her. She tried with all her might to keep her feelings of loss at bay. She had lost another crew member to a savage death. She wasn't sure how he died, only that Muziki said he saw an enormous lion. That made sense, having seen the severed foot. She tried to concentrate on the task at hand. There would be time to mourn her friend later.

Moments later, they arrived at the trail, where Raven turned left. Everyone was quiet as they followed their captain. They were stunned to see what was left of their friend, Mdago. As Raven led the way down the trail, she began to pick up the pace until she was eventually trotting. Everyone joined her as she jogged down the trail, but still, no one talked.

After ten minutes of running down the trail, Raven stopped. They entered the fifty-acre clearing, where they had been what seemed like days before. Raven stood in the clearing, watching and listening. The clearing was quiet. She saw some rhinodinos grazing at the far end to her right.

Raven decided to stay at the edge of the clearing, moving clockwise around the perimeter. It would be a less direct route, but spotting the other trail leading back to Attila would be easier. As she walked along the edge of the clearing, she became bothered by the silence. No insects were buzzing or chirping. No birds singing. It just didn't seem right.

"Everyone, keep a sharp eye out. It's too quiet."

Everyone began to realize Raven was right. It was too quiet—eerie even. The silence began to burn their ears. The only sound was their footsteps as they crunched through the dried leaves and dead grass in the clearing. They walked past a large pile of dino dung and noticed there weren't any flies buzzing around it.

A low rumble entered their ears. It came from the jungle to their left. They could smell the scent of animal fur. Raven stopped to listen. Something rustled in the brush to her left and behind her. She looked over her left shoulder. The rumble of a growl grew with intensity. Raven drew her sword from its scabbard. Everyone followed suit except Charles and Walter. They were weaponless except for their revolvers.

Raven ordered, "Everyone, spread out."

The group stepped back from each other, creating a semi-circle, with everyone facing the area from which the growling was coming. The creature leaped from the cover of the jungle into the clearing. Raven and the others stood stunned as they saw a lion the size of an elephant leap inside their semi-circle. It snarled as it landed before them, baring its long, sharp, tusk-like incisors. It had already chosen its target. It snatched up Walter, standing to the semi-circle's far right. Walter cried out in pain as the lion clutched Walter in its mouth and bit down, crushing his body. Taylor pointed his revolver at the lion and pulled the trigger six times, emptying the chambers. Every shot was accurate, hitting the lion in the side but phasing the large creature very little. The lion turned and ran back into the jungle with Walter's body hanging from its jowls, leaving everyone stunned at what they had just witnessed.

Charles Taylor cried out, "We have to go after it! We have to save Walter!"

Raven replied, "It's no use, Charles. Walter was dead the minute that lion snatched him up into its mouth. It's too fast and too dangerous for us to follow. We have to keep going."

Taylor knew she was right. But he felt terrible not being able to do anything to help his friend. He had already lost George, and now he had lost Walter, too. What would their families think when they heard their loved ones had fallen prey to prehistoric creatures? Who was he kidding? He would never make it back home. He was doomed to die on this island.

Raven led the way as they continued around the perimeter. Occasionally, Raven looked back at Charles to check on him. She saw his concern for his fallen friends. She felt his anguish because she, too, had lost several of her close friends. She felt a rush of dread and shook her head to remove the remorse. She couldn't let herself fall victim to the loss again. Her crew needed her to be strong.

They continued to trek along the edge of the clearing until Raven discovered the trail leading back into the jungle. She turned left and led her crew back toward where they had left Attila and his small band of carpenters to work on the new rudder. She had hoped to hear some of the tools being used in the distance as they walked along the path, but all she could hear was the rustling of the foliage as they traveled down the path.

Suddenly, the ground shook, and a blast erupted behind them from beyond the clearing. Raven stopped and looked back to see what was happening. She saw black smoke lifting to the sky from the top of the distant mountain. Her stomach churned as she watched. She feared the volcano might erupt at any moment, and they were running out of time. They needed to return, finish the rudder, and attach it to *Destiny* before the eruption.

They came upon a small stream about two feet wide. Raven let everyone stop for a quick rest and to refill their water skins. They each drank as much water as possible and filled their water skins. Taylor didn't have a way to carry water, so he only drank what he could while it was available. Five minutes later, they were back on the trail.

They came upon a grove of fruit trees. Mangos, oranges, and bananas were growing along their path. They each picked as much as they could and stuffed the fruits into their satchels as they walked along. Each peeled and munched on the fruit as they continued their trek through the jungle.

Hours passed as they walked through the jungle. Each person was deep in their own thoughts. Raven's mind raced from one thing to another. She thought of Jeffrey. How much she missed him already. She tried to rake the thought from her mind. She turned to her papa. She was happy he had survived. She didn't know how she could stand to lose him again. She remembered the day she once lost him in the hurricane. As she and her friends floated in the sea, she remembered thinking she would never see her papa again. She remembered how her heart ached at the thought of never seeing him and then finding him again only a few months later. How excited she was to be reunited with him.

Raven stopped. She listened to the wind as it whispered to her. A faint sound of scraping could be heard up ahead. Muffled voices spoke to each other in the distance.

She turned to the others and said, "Come on. I think we've found them."

Everyone followed Raven as she picked up the pace. She jogged along the trail as she led them toward the voices. The scraping grew louder as she trotted along. A large blue and gold macaw burst from the brush before her, startling her and causing her to balk before gathering back her wits and continuing down the path. The bird squawked as it flapped its wings and flew off to Raven's left. Her heart pounded as she felt the adrenaline flow through her.

She broke through the confines of the jungle and burst into the clearing where the large Mahogany had been cut down. Attila and his men stopped their work and hurriedly took up weapons to fight off whoever or whatever had just burst into their camp.

CHAPTER 21

Raven raised her hands in surrender and said, "Whoa, Attila! It's just us."

Attila sighed. "Raven! We thought you would never return. What took you so long?"

"We were lost. And, we lost some men."

"Yes, I lost two men to those ape-like creatures. They came again at night and took them away."

Raven replied, "Those creatures ate Bila Meno. We also lost Mdago to a large lion with long tusks. And, Jeffrey. . . Jeffrey fell into quicksand."

"I am very sorry, Raven. This island is most dangerous. We should leave as soon as possible."

"Are the boards ready for the rudder?"

"Aye! We have four good, long, straight boards. We can finish them on the ship."

Raven said to everyone, "Let's get going. Maybe we can be on the ship by nightfall."

Everyone packed up their gear and fell into line to trek back to the beach. The eight men who remained with Attila took up the new planks, two men per board, and followed along the path. Raven led the way while Attila and Kifaru brought up the rear of the procession. Raven kept a moderate pace, eager to return to *Destiny* but not wanting to tire her men out too quickly. No one spoke as they traveled down the path leading to the beach. The only sounds they heard were the crunching of their footsteps in the sand, the birds chirping in the trees, and the insects buzzing.

The day seemed hotter and more humid than previous days on the island, making walking along the path more challenging. No breeze stirred to cool their bodies. Sweat ran down their faces as they traveled down the path, and perspiration soaked their clothes, making it uncomfortable to walk through the jungle. Raven opened up her waistcoat to gain some relief from the tight-fitting leather. Her beautiful, long red curls had become a frizzled mass of locks.

After an hour, Raven announced, "Let's rest for a moment."

The men hauling the long planks dropped them to the ground with great relief. Others allowed themselves to drop to their knees as they pulled out their waterskins to take a sip.

Suddenly, the ground began to shake. Everyone reached for the nearest tree to help steady themselves as the ground vibrated beneath them. Coconuts and mangos fell from the tops of nearby trees, plummeting to the ground like cannonballs. Monkeys screeched in terror as their trees shook. Birds took flight to escape the violent shaking of the trees. Larger animals could be seen and heard rushing through the jungle, trying to escape the unknown force, causing their island home to convulse beneath their feet.

Attila heard large creatures running toward them from behind, panicked by the earthquake. He saw trees falling to the ground as the creatures crashed against them, trying to escape the unknown.

"Raven! We have to get moving! The giant animals are heading our way!"

Everyone hopped to their feet and followed Raven as she ran down the path toward the beach. The men carrying the planks found it difficult to carry their load while running, but they ran as best they could.

Attila glanced over his shoulder from time to time and saw tall trees falling to the ground as large animals crashed through them, trying to escape. He heard the frightened cries of the dinosaurs as they crashed through the jungle. Attila saw a group of rhinodinos on his left flank as they crashed through a grove of mangoes. Fruit flew into the air as trees were knocked down and left overturned in the wake of the massive creatures.

Monkeys scattered through the trees, screeching as the trees shook from the giant lizard knocking them down. A rexysaur roared its displeasure at the mountain, which was spewing smoke into the air and causing the ground to quake beneath its feet. The rexy rumbled on two feet, pushing trees aside, making a new path for itself. The whole island was enwrapped in chaos.

Raven's crew ran, searching for the beach where they had hoped to find safety. The arms of the eight who carried the rudder boards were aching and burning, longing for relief. They stumbled through the jungle, their chests heaving in pain as they gasped for air.

Raven's feet felt weighted as she ran through the jungle path. She wondered to herself, "*Will this turmoil never end?*"

Suddenly, the ground became more difficult to run across. The ground cover diminished until they were running only on dry sand.

"The beach is up ahead! We're almost there!"

Raven and her crew exploded from the jungle and landed on the sand twenty feet from the ocean. Raven looked around as she lay in the sand and saw various kinds of wildlife scattered along the shoreline. To her left was a herd of rhinodinos, and to her right was a rexysaur about fifty yards away. The rexy wasn't concerned about them. It seemed more concerned about the danger that lay behind them all. Numerous types of creatures exited the jungle, many of which Raven had not yet seen. They all scattered about on the beach, but none of them attacked each other or the humans. They all seemed more concerned with something more dangerous than each other.

Attila took his men to the boats, still tied up near the tree line. They untied the dories and dragged them to the beach's edge so they could be launched. They dragged the four hand-carved boards to the dories and tied two to each one of the dories. Everyone climbed into the dories and began to row back to *Destiny*. When they reached the halfway point back to the ship, they heard a loud explosion coming from the island. They turned back to see what it was. The top of the mountain had blown up, and dirt, rock, and lava were scattered into the sky at unbelievable heights.

The explosion sprayed hot molten lava so far into the sky that the trajectory sent it as far out as the beach and even into the ocean. The fiery rain spilled all around Raven and her crew as they rowed back to the ship. They tried to dodge the burning stones that fell upon them, but there were too many. The molten stones fell into the dories, hitting and burning the crew as they fled the island. One burning stone landed in Raven's hair and singed it before John could rake it from her head. He burned his hand as he wiped the stone away and threw it into the water.

Red-hot coals landed in the boats and ignited the wooden hulls. The men cupped their hands into the sea and scooped up water to extinguish the fires. They also used the water to extinguish the burns on their skin from the burning hailstones. Raven faced the rear of the boat she was a passenger in and noticed what was happening on the beach. The falling lava rocks struck several of the Dinos. Some were on fire and running across the beach in a panic. Others ran back into the jungle, trying to hide from the hail. Many of the smaller creatures lay dead and burning on the sand at the edge of the jungle.

Raven and the dories reached the ship and threw their ropes up to the crew remaining on *Destiny*. While Raven and John climbed back onto the ship, the rest of her crew remained to pass the four rudder boards up to the ship's deck. Attila and Charles Taylor followed soon after Raven and John. Once Raven was onboard the ship, she ran to the quarterdeck and pulled out her spyglass from her satchel. She pointed it back to the mountain and watched as fire and smoke plumed from the mountaintop. Lava began to flow from the top of the mountain and run down its sides, overflowing into the jungle. The mountain continued to explode, one blast after another. It was as if the mountain was determined to obliterate the island.

Sean O'Toole suddenly stood by her side, "What is it, lass?"

"The volcano! It seems to be erupting. We need to get away as soon as we can."

Raven turned and left Sean standing alone as she went to check on her crew, which was loading the planks onto the ship.

They moved the rudder boards onto *Destiny* so Mr. Greer could complete the repairs. Kifaru, Muziki, Mtamu, and Mvuvi were still in the dories, ready to attach the ropes that would lift them up to the ship.

A long, slippery tentacle rose from the sea and wrapped itself around Kifaru. He screamed for help, and Raven turned just in time to see the giant sea creature take him underwater. Another tentacle reached over the side of the other dory and grabbed Mvuvi. Mvuvi took out his knife and stabbed the creature over and over, trying to free himself of the slimy, eel-like arms of the unknown aquatic being. Blood spurted from the sea creature's arm wrapped around Mvuvi. He was determined not to allow this creature to drag him down with Kifaru. He slashed and cut with all his might until the arm released him. Slowly, the injured arm slid back into the water and disappeared.

Mvuvi called the crew onboard Destiny, "Pull me up!"

The crew tugged against the ropes attached to pulleys that raised the dory onto the ship. Mvuvi staggered out of the boat and fell into the arms of his fellow crewmates. He breathed heavily and said to them, "Thank you."

Raven called to those holding onto Mvuvi, "Get him below. He needs rest."

Mvuvi's mates carried him below and placed him into his hammock.

Andrew Greer and his carpenters took the newly made boards below to construct and install the new rudder. Raven went to her quarters. As she opened the door and walked in, Captain Billings screeched his delight and jumped onto her shoulder, almost knocking Raven over. She hugged the monkey and said, "Oh, I missed you, too."

Raven carried the captain to her bed, where she collapsed and fell asleep. Captain Billings nestled himself in her curls and rummaged through her hair, looking for ticks or lice he might eat.

John Ashworth walked over to where Charles Taylor was standing and asked, "Would you like to get some rest?"

"Rest would be nice."

"Come along then. I'll show you to a hammock you can use."

John took him below and found an unused hammock. Taylor slid into the swinging bed and twisted and turned until he found a comfortable position. He looked at John and said, "Thanks, this will do nicely."

John turned and walked away, then climbed back to the main deck.

Everyone from the landing crew found their beds and collapsed for the night. They were hungry but too tired to eat.

CHAPTER 22

Jeremy had the night watch. He and a few of the crew kept watch over the ship while everyone else slept. Mr. Greer and his carpenters had retired for the night before finishing the installation of the new rudder. Many of the boards had been cut to the proper size and even joined with tongue and groove connections, but not all of them. Once they had added the last of the boards, they would still need to thread the ropes through the steering pulleys to operate the rudder properly.

Jeremy stood near the helm on the quarterdeck and used his spyglass to examine the horizon in every direction. Mtamu stood in the crow's nest, searching the horizon for any vessels that might approach and any creatures that might try to attack from the mysterious island.

The island seemed quiet for the moment. The mountain at the center of the island seemed dormant for now. The sky was clear, with the stars shining brightly at night, although Jeremy didn't recognize any of the stars that appeared above him. The moon was in complete phase, but it, too, seemed odd. The heavenly body that usually glowed white in the sky was more of a sepia tint. The sight of it disturbed Jeremy.

Jeremy walked over to *Destiny's* bell and rang it four times, indicating 2:00 a.m. In two more hours, John Ashworth would relieve him at the watch. Jeremy yawned and wiped his eyes to remove the sleep from them.

Someone moved on the main deck, startling Jeremy. He waited to see who it might be. When the shadow moved toward the quarterdeck, Jeremy found the silhouette familiar. It was Raven. She climbed the steps to the quarterdeck and joined Jeremy.

"Not able to sleep?"

"Not really."

"Why not?"

"Too much has happened. There's too much on my mind."

"It's Jeffrey, isn't it?"

Raven stood quietly as tears formed in the corners of her eyes.

"I'm sorry, Raven. I know you and he were very close. I hope you don't mind if I ask. How did it happen?"

Raven sniffled and replied, "We were all running, trying to escape a massive creature chasing anything and everything through a clearing in the middle of the island. Everyone scattered into the jungle, trying to escape the giant creature. I tried to follow Jeffrey through the jungle, but we became separated. Then, I heard him. I followed the direction of his call, which led me to a small clearing where I found him submerged in quicksand. I couldn't reach him. I tried to find something to reach him so I could pull him out, but it was useless. He was gone."

"How horrible for you, Raven. I'm so sorry he's gone. I, too, was quite fond of him."

The two of them stood quietly together for a while.

Soon afterward, John walked to the quarterdeck and stood by his daughter. He slipped his arm around her shoulder and pulled her close to him. She put her arm around his waist.

"This all feels like a bad dream, Papa. I can't believe Jeffrey is gone. Everything we experienced on this island is so unbelievable. I just want to wake up and have it all be over with."

"I know, Raven. You've already experienced so much loss these past few years, but you'll get through it. You always do."

Raven sniffled as the tears began to roll down her cheeks once again. She gripped her papa all the more, trying to overcome her agony of loss.

Jeremy excused himself from the quarterdeck to leave them alone. His watch was over, and John's was beginning. John glanced at the hourglass and saw that time was running out. He released his grip on Raven, walked over to the glass, and turned it over before ringing the bell eight times.

More crew members began climbing onto the main deck, ready to begin their workday. Mr. Greer appeared on deck and waved to Raven and John standing on the quarterdeck. He called over his crew of carpenters to assist him in installing the new rudder.

The green sunlight lit up the sky with an eerie tint of sage. Raven looked back at the island and noticed the sun rising over the peak of the fiery mountain, which was once again erupting. Birds scattered from the mountain and flew, radiating away from the volcano in all directions.

Suddenly, something exploded into the sky from the top of the mountain, followed by more fiery hailstones. Raven heard an eerie screech from the mountain that echoed throughout the island and beyond. A creature living inside the mountain was now on the loose. It looked like a large bird from Raven's point of view. But, instead of a feathery tail, the animal had a long tail like a lizard or a snake.

Raven took out her spyglass to have a closer look. She was right. The creature didn't have feathers at all. It had scales that shimmered in the sunlight, much like fish scales. The being had leathery wings that flapped violently through the air, carrying the creature high above the mountain. As it circled the mountain, Raven could see it wasn't birdlike at all, except that it was flying. It had four legs; its front legs were much shorter than the rear legs. Each foot appeared to be outfitted with razor-sharp talons. The beast's chest was covered with scales resembling chain mail from her vantage point. Its eyes sparkled red in the green sunlight.

Once it had escaped the mountain, the creature began flying around the island in a circular motion, hunting for something unknown to Raven.

John heard Raven gasp.

"What is it, Raven?"

Raven said nothing, passing her spyglass over to John for him to see for himself. John looked through the eyepiece and said, "Bleeding barnacles, what is that!"

He looked back at Raven, shocked by what he had witnessed.

Raven replied, "I hope it is a mirage, but it looks like what I've heard called a dragon."

"A dragon? But I thought they were all gone centuries ago, if they ever existed in the first place."

"Aye, Papa. But this island had been full of surprises. I can't say that I'm exactly shocked by this."

Raven pulled out her conch shell and blasted the alarm for all hands. Men scrambled to the main deck from below, many of them half-dressed as they stumbled from the ladder to the main deck. They all searched the waters, expecting to see an approaching vessel that might be ready to attack *Destiny*. They were puzzled when no ship could be seen in any direction around them.

Raven called them to gather just below the quarterdeck so she could give them instructions. Jeremy was the last man to arrive, having fallen asleep just moments before.

"Arm yourselves! Make ready the deck guns! A dragon appears to be heading this way from the island."

"A dragon?"

"What's a dragon?"

Several of the Africans threw questions out to the winds, having never heard of a dragon.

Jeremy barked his orders to the gun crew.

"Load all cannons, men! Everyone, ready your rifles and pistols."

Someone called out, "What is a dragon?"

Jeremy replied, "If it truly is a dragon, it will be a fierce flying beast that breathes fire. No one in our lifetime has ever seen one. There are legends about them in my country. They are nearly impossible to kill. Now, get your guns ready!"

Raven watched the creature through her spyglass as it circled the island, expanding its circumference outward toward the sea. As she watched, she realized the creature was far larger than any animal she had ever seen. Even larger than the megasaur she had seen on the island, which had terrified everything in its path.

Suddenly, the beast swooped down toward the jungle floor and disappeared. Then it flew back into the air carrying something in its front talons. Raven looked through her glass again and watched the creature fly back to the mountain carrying a rexysaur with its front feet. Raven was so stunned by the dragon's immense size that it could easily carry away the massive dinosaur.

She called her men to stand down when she realized the dragon was returning to its den somewhere deep in the island's mountain. Jeremy had his gun crew sweep out the already loaded cannons and secure them to the decks for travel if they could ever get the rudder installed.

Charles Taylor joined Raven and John on the quarterdeck, breathing heavily as he approached them.

"Was that a dragon?"

Raven replied, "I don't know. I've never seen a dragon. I've only heard stories passed down from the elderly about them. I've always thought them to be stories made up to entertain children."

"Well, entertaining isn't the word I would use to describe it. More like terrifying."

Raven remarked, "We need to install that rudder and get out of here before that... thing returns."

John said, "I'll check with Hardy and see if we need any supplies before we launch."

Attila joined Raven and Taylor on the quarterdeck and asked, "What are your orders?"

"Mr. Ashworth is checking on our supply status. Would you please see how the new rudder is coming along? I want us to leave this island as soon as possible."

"Aye, Raven."

Attila went below decks to find Mr. Greer and his crew of carpenters working on the new rudder.

"Mr. Greer, Raven would like a report of your progress, please."

Greer looked back to see who was asking such an impertinent question. When he saw it was Attila, his countenance changed as he replied, "Oh, Attila, it's you. Well, we're still attaching the new rudder, and then we will have to rethread the steering ropes. Some of the ropes are frayed and will have to be replaced, so it will be at least the end of the day before we can sail, if then."

"Is there anything we can do to help?"

Andrew shook his head in disgust. "No, no. It's just going to take time. We can't rush things. If we want to get out of here and survive, we must do things right. We will make haste, but not to the detriment of *Destiny*. We want her to get us out of here successfully now, don't we?"

"Aye, Mr. Greer."

Attila climbed back up to the quarterdeck and reported all Mr. Greer had said to Raven.

Just as he finished his report, John Ashworth returned to the quarter-deck and reported, "Raven, I'm afraid I have some bad news."

"What is it, Mr. Ashworth?"

"Mr. Hardy reports that our fresh water supply is running low. We need to go back to that blasted island and get more water."

Raven sighed. "Alright, I'll assemble a crew and return to resupply the water. What about food supplies?"

John replied, "He says we have plenty for now."

"Alright, Attila, you'll take command of the ship while Mr. Ashworth and I go ashore."

"Aye, Raven."

CHAPTER 23

Raven and John selected a crew of ten men to take ten water barrels back onto the island and fill them with water from one of the freshwater streams. Charles Taylor offered to help guard the men as they went to and from the stream. Raven armed Taylor with two pistols, a long gun, and his six-shot revolver to help guard the crew. Raven and all her crew were heavily armed as well.

They landed on the beach using two dories to haul the empty barrels. Raven led the way down the path they had previously cleared. John and Charles brought up the rear while Raven's ten crew members rolled their barrels along the path. The path followed a slight upward incline as they traveled through the jungle. Pushing the barrels up this path was strenuous, but not as much as it would have been trying to roll them uphill back to the beach while filled, had the incline been in the opposite direction. The downward slope coming back would be a bit of a relief. Their primary concern would be keeping the barrels from rolling downhill too quickly on the return.

Rolling the barrels up the path leading to the stream was back-breaking work. Constantly bending over while pushing a heavy barrel taxed the crew's bodies. Raven tried to ease their burdens by allowing them a five-minute break once in a while. The men stood straight and stretched their back muscles, reaching their hands toward the sky to find relief. After their break, they continued up the path.

Two hours later, they found a shallow stream crossing the path they had been traveling. The waterway was about twelve feet wide and only two feet deep at its deepest point. They rolled the barrels into the stream, uncorked a hole in the top of each barrel, and dipped the opened hole beneath the water's surface to allow the barrel to fill. The water wasn't deep enough to submerge the barrels completely, so they could not fill them to the top. After allowing as much water to enter the barrels as possible, they replaced the cork in the tap hole and rolled the barrel out of the stream. The barrels were much heavier now, requiring four men to roll the barrels back onto the bank of the stream.

Once they finished filling all ten barrels, Raven led the way back down the path toward the beach. She strolled, allowing the men pushing the barrels to move at their own pace. Sometimes, she had to walk faster as they made a descent. Sometimes, each man placed himself in front of the barrel to keep it from rolling too fast down a sharp decline.

Halfway down the path, the ground began to shake, and the mountain once again began to rumble. Fire and ash spewed from the top of the mountain, billowing smoke toward the cloudless sky. Wildlife throughout the jungle panicked, fleeing in all directions, some heading toward the beach while others scattered to the opposite side of the island. Birds took flight, filling the sky with clouds of winged silhouettes.

Raven's heart raced as she searched the area for any of the larger creatures that might be fleeing in their direction. She was frightened that she and her crew might be in the path of a stampede of giant Dino-creatures.

Raven heard a bone-chilling screech far in the distance. As she peeked over her left shoulder, she witnessed what she feared most: a winged reptile flying out of the top of the mountain once more. The dragon flew straight up far above the mountain peak before leveling off and circling the mountaintop.

"Alright, everyone! We need to move faster!"

John asked from the back of the line, "What is it, Raven?"

She pointed to the sky and cried out, "LOOK!"

Everyone stopped to see what Raven was pointing to. They panicked when they saw the dragon flying and circling the mountain. Every man rolled the barrels as fast as they could down the path back to the beach. Raven led the way, glancing back occasionally to ensure they weren't being followed.

They were about halfway back to their destination when Raven noticed the dragon's circle was increasing as it flew around the mountain. It was evident to her that the creature was hunting for its next meal.

"I know you men are tired, but we've got to go faster."

Each man dug deep within himself to find the needed strength to roll the barrels faster. They gasped for air as their arms ached and their legs burned. Still, the fear of being a dragon's next dinner kept them moving forward.

The dragon's screeches grew louder as the dragon flew closer. The closer it came, the better look Raven had at the giant lizard. She could see its eyes were red like fire. Its shimmering scales along its back were emerald colored, and those along its belly were violet. The talons at the end of each of its toes were sharp and pointed like a pike.

Raven realized the dragon was drawing nearer with each trip around the island. She decided they would need to change strategy and not depend on trying to outrun the creature alone. She instructed her men, "Be ready! When I tell you to, leave your barrels on the trail and hide in the brush. We'll travel only when the dragon is flying away from us."

Raven continued to watch the dragon as it circled the island, widening its path. As it came back toward them, Raven shouted, "Hide!"

All of her men ducked into the jungle to hide from the giant that soared above them. Raven noticed the dragon was much larger than she could have imagined as it flew above her. She thought it to be at least twice the size of a full-grown rexysaur. Its leathery wings expanded a width twice as long as *Destiny*. Raven couldn't fathom how an enormous creature could stay in flight. As it flew over them, it let out a scream that almost shattered their eardrums. Raven cupped her hands over her ears to help relieve the sharp shrill that entered her brain.

Once the dragon flew past, Raven called her men to return to the barrels. They rolled down the slight incline leading to the beach with greater fervor, realizing how close they had come to the monstrous creature. Each man was more determined now to escape the jungle before the dragon could make another swipe across their path.

Attila stood on the quarterdeck as he witnessed the dragon flying nearer and nearer to their location at the shore's edge. Jeremy and his gun crew had just finished swabbing out and clearing the tubes of their cannons when Attila called out, "Jeremy! Man your guns! The creature has returned, and it is coming closer this time!"

Jeremy ordered his men, "You heard him! Ready the guns!"

The crew scrambled again, loading the cannons with new shot and gunpowder. Jeremy moved to the starboard side facing the island while the ship was anchored offshore. He decided on an elevation and instructed his men to adjust the cannon to the correct angle. Jeremy thought he knew which path Raven and her crew would take to return to the beach and wanted to ensure his shots fired wide of their mark. He took out his spyglass and watched the dragon fly around the island. Then he swung it back toward the jungle to search for Raven.

Attila ordered, "Don't fire until I give the order."

"Aye, Captain Attila!"

The crew waited as Attila and Jeremy searched the area, waiting for Raven to appear from the jungle onto the beach. The dragon made another pass across the beach as it circled the island, looking for prey. It roared again with a mighty screech that pierced everyone's hearing. Then, it continued past the landing area to the island's backside.

Suddenly, Raven and her crew appeared on the beach, rolling the water barrels over the sand to reach the dories before the dragon returned to find them. They struggled through the sand, trying to roll the heavy barrels to the boats.

Raven ordered, "Work together and carry the barrels to the boats rather than trying to roll them through the sand."

Her men grouped in teams of four, carrying the barrels while staggering through the deep sand. John and Charles Taylor helped carry with the third team as Raven watched over them all.

Walking through the sand was most difficult, even with four men at each barrel. As they carried the barrels, the water inside sloshed from side to side, causing the barrels to move and work against the men as they carried them. It was like being tossed by the waves of the ocean.

The first team reached the first dory and struggled as they placed the barrel inside the boat. Moments later, the next barrel arrived, and the first team began their trip back to the remaining barrels. The third team was right behind the second team but moved to the second dory to place their barrel inside it.

Raven's anxiety was high as adrenaline rushed through her body. She kept her eyes toward the sky, searching to her left, expecting the dragon to continue its counterclockwise direction as it flew over the island. She hadn't seen the dragon for several minutes but could still hear the faint sound of its screech somewhere on the island's far side.

"Hurry!" she cried.

The first team slogged past her with the fourth barrel and placed it inside the second dory. Four of the ten barrels were now loaded.

"You're doing well, men, but you must hurry even more."

The second team trudged past her with the fifth barrel and placed it inside the first dory. Team three was right on their heels and placed their barrel into the second dory. Just as they finished, Raven spotted the dragon moving toward them again.

"Everyone! Move back into the jungle! The dragon is coming again!"

Team one had already started with their next barrel but set it down and ran toward the jungle. Everyone else retreated past them and hid just inside the tree line, hoping the dragon wouldn't spot them.

Raven turned to John, who stood beside her, and asked, "I wonder what it's looking for?"

"Something to eat, I would expect."

"No. I think it's hunting us. There are plenty of animals to feed on here on this island. It could have had any one of them by now. It keeps circling the island as if looking for something other than its next meal."

"Well, let's just make sure we aren't its next meal," John replied.

The dragon flew past them again, but it was much lower to the ground this time. Raven measured it to be only fifty feet above the beach as it flew by them. Then, the dragon stretched its head back upward and flew higher again.

Raven stepped out of the jungle and watched the dragon fly away again. "Hurry! Let's get these last barrels loaded."

The men scrambled back onto the beach and picked up the barrels as they struggled again through the sand. Nine barrels were now loaded and ready to go. Raven sent half the crew with the first dory back to the ship while the last crew returned for the final barrel.

Six men pulled on the oars, sending the boat through the waves, while one man sat at the rudder to steer them back to *Destiny*. The others remained behind to help load the final barrel. John and Charles stood by to guard them as they carried the last barrel across the sand.

Just as they reached the dory, the dragon appeared behind them, flying over the treetops in a different direction than it had taken before. The dragon startled them all as it let out another of its ear-piercing screams. The four men carrying the barrel lost their grips and dropped it into the sand, shy of the boat. They struggled to regain their composure but finally loaded the barrel into the boat.

A blast came from *Destiny* as Jeremy's gunmen fired one of the cannons. Raven saw the cannonball arch through the sky toward their beach before it fell into the jungle, missing the flying lizard by at least twenty feet.

Raven fired both her pistols at the giant flying lizard. She hit the animal with both shots, but the lead seemed to bounce off the creature's scales like pebbles being repelled by armor. John raised his long gun and fired, aiming for the dragon's head, but missed. The dragon raised itself up and flapped its wings to hover above them all. It chose its target and swooped down to collect it. Charles Taylor fired once with his long gun and tossed it away as he reached for the two pistols he carried in his belt. He fired both pistols at the dragon as it flew toward him. The dragon reached out with its front talons, snatched Taylor from the ground, and carried him away.

Taylor screamed in pain as the dragon clinched its talons deep into Taylor's body.

Raven cried out, "No!" as she watched Taylor being carried away back toward the volcanic mountain.

Three more cannon shots rang out from the ship, but all three shots missed their target. The dragon was gone, and so was Taylor.

Chapter 24

A s they returned to *Destiny*, Raven mourned the man she had only recently met. She knew very little of him, but she mourned anyway. Raven hated to see anyone die in such a fashion, but this island seemed determined to take any human who found it. She had seen more death on this little island than on any other island she had visited, by tenfold at least. She was determined that Charles Taylor would be the last to be taken from her by this God-forsaken island.

They reached the ship, unloaded the water barrels, and secured them below decks. Raven asked Jeremy to find Mr. Greer and have him report on the status of their repair. Jeremy climbed below to the second deck and moved toward the stern to find Mr. Greer still overseeing the installation of the new rudder.

"Mr. Greer, the captain sends her compliments and requests a report on your status."

"Mr. Finch, tell Raven all should be finished within the hour."

"Aye, Mr. Greer. Well done, sir."

Jeremy left Mr. Greer, climbed back up to the main deck, and found Raven on the quarterdeck to report.

"Captain, Mr. Greer reports that the repairs will be finished within the hour."

"Very good, Jeremy. Have the crew prepare to make sail as soon as the repairs are finished."

"Aye, Raven."

Raven was exhausted and longed to see her bed, but with the repairs so close to completion, she was determined to remain above decks to get the ship moving as soon as Mr. Greer gave word that *Destiny* was ready.

Raven could never tell what time it was here by the sun's position. It seemed the sun rose and set by its own whims. It might be in the sky for three hours or hang aloft for twenty hours. The ship's bell was the only way they had to keep time. If it had not been for the watchman, time would not exist here.

A strong wind began to blow away from the island. This gave Raven hope that they would soon be far from here. She walked to the stern and pulled out her spyglass to have another look at the troublesome island that had held them captive for so long and had devastated her crew. She felt that only the devil himself could be responsible for creating such an island as this. Raven scanned the beach, then turned her glass toward the mountain that seemed unusually quiet at the moment. John walked up and joined her.

"What is it, daughter?"

"That blasted mountain has done nothing but rumble and shake and spit fire the whole time we've been here. I'm wondering why it is so quiet now."

John sighed, "Maybe it's just tired... or maybe it's the calm before the real storm that is about to hit us."

"I hope it's your prior suggestion. I could do with a little piece of quiet right now."

"Aye, my heart has been racing every minute since we arrived here. I look forward to returning to the Robin's Nest, where we can relax for a while."

As they both stood and looked back at the island, Raven noticed a fin appear in the water below them.

"Look, Papa. Is that a shark?"

"Well, if it is, it's the largest shark I've ever seen."

The fin grew larger and taller as the fish swam closer to the surface. Suddenly, the fin stood four feet out of the water. They could see the shark's length as it swam near the surface and were amazed to see how long it was.

"Papa, it's half the length of *Destiny*."

"Aye, I have never seen a shark anywhere near as long as this. It's more like a whale than a shark."

The shark moved back and forth down the ship's length as if searching for something. At one point, it passed along the anchor chain and rubbed against it, causing the ship to rock from side to side. Everyone on deck had to brace to keep from falling over. Raven grabbed the rail as the ship rocked. The shark continued pacing through the water but moved closer with each turn. The shark made another trip alongside the ship, this time rubbing against *Destiny's* length, causing her to list to the port. Everyone scrambled to find a hold to keep from falling over the rail into the water.

Raven told John, "We've got to get rid of that fish before it takes down the ship."

She ran to the helm and looked out over the deck to find Jeremy. He was just stepping out of the hatch that led to below decks.

"Jeremy! Fire your guns at that shark before it takes us down!"

Jeremy ran to the rail to see what Raven was talking about. There, he saw the giant fish swimming against the vessel's side, causing it to list.

"It's too close to hit it with cannon fire; we'll have to use the long guns!"

Raven replied, "Alright! Snap to!"

Jeremy's gunmen took up their long guns and aimed into the water at the giant beast swimming the length of *Destiny*.

"Fire at will!"

The gunmen fired their shots at the shark as it swam past each man. Each shot hit its mark but seemed to do little to no damage to the determined beast.

"Reload!"

Each man reloaded his weapon and prepared to fire again.

"Aim!"

Before Jeremy could give the order to fire, a much larger creature appeared from the ocean depths and swallowed the shark in one bite. The power of its entry back below the water's surface caused *Destiny* to list even more than before. Everyone aboard the ship scrambled for the nearest handhold to avoid being tossed into the drink. *Destiny* took on water as if she had been in a severe hurricane. Raven was afraid she might sink.

"Quick! Man the bilge pumps!"

Four men ran for the hatch leading to the second deck and disappeared from sight as they ran to operate the pumps that would expel the excess water from *Destiny's* lower decks. Just as they dropped into the hatch, Mr. Greer came above decks in a tizzy.

"What in blue blazes is going on?!"

Raven replied from the quarterdeck, "A giant shark was attacking us. It listed the ship as it rubbed against our hull. Another larger fish appeared and swallowed the shark. It almost turned us over with the force of its dive back into the water."

Greer announced, "Ah, yes. There's always a bigger fish, isn't there?"

"Mr. Greer, am I to assume that the steerage is now repaired?"

"Aye, Raven. She's ready whenever you are."

"Well done."

Raven turned to John and said, "Let's get underway. I want to leave this island immediately."

"Aye, Raven."

John ordered all hands to make ready to sail. Several of the crew moved to the capstan and began turning it to raise the anchor out of the water where it had been resting at the bottom of the sea. Everyone else ran to their stations on deck to prepare the sails for launch. Men climbed the rigging and began unfurling the sails to drop from the yardarms to catch the wind. No sooner had they climbed into place than the wind disappeared. The sails dropped into place but hung listlessly. Everyone looked at Raven standing on the quarterdeck as she looked at the sails, waiting for the wind to return and carry them away.

She waited. Nothing happened.

She gritted her teeth and said with a clenched jaw, "I can't believe it. We finally get ready to leave, and the wind leaves us."

John knowingly shook his head, "It's as if somebody doesn't want us to leave this island."

Jeremy's men came down from the masts with puzzled faces. Mvuvi remained in the crow's nest to watch for any signs of the wind returning.

John asked his daughter, "What would you have us do?"

"Drop the anchor again. Set up the watch. Send everyone else to their bunks. If the wind returns, muster the crews. I'm exhausted. I'm going to bed."

"Aye, Raven."

Raven stepped into her quarters and found Captain Billings resting on her bed, munching on a banana. She removed her boots and coat, unbuttoned her waistcoat, and collapsed onto her bed. The captain moved to her face and offered her a bite of his banana.

"No thanks. I'm too tired to eat."

John stood at the helm, watching the horizon in all directions. The green sun hovered in the sky, not moving as he watched hour after hour. The watch bell rang each turn of the hourglass for twenty-four turns without the sun changing its position in the sky. Instead of lowering itself, it seemed to radiate more intensely with no wind to give them relief from its heat.

Attila finally came and relieved John from the watch.

"What say you, John?"

"This blasted sun is intending to drive us all mad. It hasn't moved in over twelve hours from that spot in the sky. No wind. No relief."

"Don't worry, John. I will pray to Mungu to send us rain. He will help us leave this island. You go and get some rest. This might take a while. Sometimes, Mungu expects us to be patient."

"Yeah, well, Mungu and this island are trying my patience."

Attila shook his head and smiled as John walked away.

Another twelve hours passed, and the sun had not moved. Hadari had relieved Attila at the watch four hours earlier, and he, like John, was tiring of the heat that beat down on them from the sun that had seemed to have frozen in place.

Raven joined Hadari at the helm after a long and restful sleep. She couldn't remember ever having twelve hours of uninterrupted sleep.

"Hadari, how many times has the sun set since I left the deck?"

"None, Raven. The sun is determined not to leave us."

Raven sighed. She looked around the ship and saw her men milling around. Many of them leaned against the rail, visiting with one another. They were bored, having never experienced so much downtime since they had come to sail with Raven.

Seven days had passed, and the sun had still not set. The wind was nonexistent. However, the mountain began to rumble once more. It had been dormant since the last appearance of the dragon, but now it was as if it were waking from a week-long sleep.

The rumbling intensified over time before fire exploded from the mountaintop. Smoke billowed from the crest, and the island began to shake visibly. Raven watched the mountain's smoke, ash, and fire display for at least an hour when lava began seeping from the top and pouring out onto the island. Raven watched as birds took flight, trying to escape the lava and fireballs that exploded from the volcano. Animals could be heard as they panicked throughout the jungle, not knowing where they could run to escape.

Raven looked through her spyglass and saw the dragon escape the mouth of the volcano once more. Even at the distance from where she watched, Raven could hear the screech of the flying reptile. She watched as the dragon hovered above the mountain, directing his attention toward Raven's ship. Then, instead of taking its usual flight path circling the island, the dragon flew toward *Destiny*.

"Jeremy! Man the guns! The dragon has returned!"

Chapter 25

The dragon flew toward the ship resting in the bay. His screeches grew louder as he approached the disabled ship. Raven searched the skies all around, wondering, "*Where is the wind?*"

Then she called out, "Jeremy, are the guns ready?!"

"Aye, Raven!"

"Don't let that creature get anywhere near my ship!"

The starboard guns were facing the island, and the massive monster was heading toward them. Jeremy wanted to wound the dragon, at least before it came close enough to attack. He had heard that dragons could breathe fire, but no one had seen a dragon before, at least no one he had ever known, so he wasn't sure if it was true.

Jeremy aimed with the starboard bow gun, raising it enough to reach the calculated distance.

"Fire!" he called.

"Boom!"

The shot rang out as smoke billowed from the cylinder, sending the iron ball through the air. Jeremy watched to see if he would hit his target. His aim seemed accurate, but the dragon soared above the cannonball's path at the last moment and escaped death.

"Reload!"

Jeremy's men scrambled, swabbing out the cannon and reloading it for its next attempt.

"Make ready all starboard guns!"

Jeremy's crew loaded all the starboard cannons and prepared to fire when ordered. Jeremy instructed his men, "Cannon one, make your elevation 20º. Cannon two, elevation 18º. Cannon three, elevation 22º. Cannon four, 19º. We're going to try to corral it with our shots."

Everyone prepared their cannons and waited for Jeremy's order. The dragon continued on its course toward *Destiny*. Jeremy intended to wait until the dragon was close enough that the quick succession of cannon fire would be difficult to react to. It didn't take long for the dragon to reach the half-mile mark Jeremy had set in his head.

"Line up your shots, men!"

Jeremy held his breath as he waited for the last moment.

"Fire one!"

"Fire two!"

"Fire three!"

Boom! Boom! Boom!

The three shots exploded in succession toward the dragon; it barely had time to react, but react it did. He spread his wings out to stop in mid-air as if applying his brakes.

Boom!

The fourth cannon exploded its shot and hit the dragon in the chest in less than a second. The dragon repelled in mid-air as if it had hit an invisible wall. It cried out in pain and anger with an even more horrific screech, like metal scraping against metal.

"Reload your guns!"

Jeremy's men were already ahead of him, swabbing out the cannons and replacing the shot and powder.

"Aim and fire when ready!"

Cannon one was ready within seconds and fired at the dragon. This time, the cannonball hit the dragon in his right wing near his shoulder, blowing a hole through his wing. The dragon screeched in pain again. Cannon three's shot flew and caught the dragon in his right hind quarter, breaking his leg. Cannon two and four shot simultaneously, hitting the dragon in his chest. The impact of both cannonballs hitting him knocked him backward in the sky and knocked out his breath. The dragon fell from the sky and landed with a thud that shook the island.

The mighty creature gasped for air but only managed a cough or two. Raven watched him as he lay on the ground, looking at him through her spyglass. His eyes were closed, and his breathing was labored.

Jeremy's men erupted in cheers of victory as they saw the fallen dragon lying in the sand.

Jeremy ran to Raven and asked, "Shall we go ashore and finish it off?"

"I think not, Jeremy. For all we know, that creature might explode into flames at any moment. We'll wait to see if he can get up again before we attack."

Raven continued to watch the creature through her spyglass. She searched the surrounding areas to ensure that nothing else was nearby that might attack them. It seemed as if the whole island was at a standstill.

Nothing moved.

The birds weren't singing; the monkeys didn't chatter.

Raven looked back at the dragon lying on the sand. Smoke billowed from his nostrils. She noticed his red eyes were drooping, almost closed. He blinked, trying to force them open. Finally, his eyes shut. His labored breathing had ended. No more smoke escaped his nostrils.

Raven turned to her crew and announced, "He's dead!"

Cheers erupted from the crew as they raised their hands in victory and congratulated one another. They had beaten the mighty dragon. Sir

Lancelot and King Arthur would be proud of them, Raven thought. No one else would believe them, should the story be told.

"Now, if we can only get away from this cursed island," she thought.

Then, Raven noticed something: the sun was starting to lower. It dropped almost like a string holding it up in the sky had broken. The sun lowered behind the horizon, exposing them to instantaneous darkness. And dark it was. The moon failed to appear in place of the sun. No stars shone in the night sky. It was total ethereal darkness.

"Light the lamps," Raven ordered.

Her men scrambled to light the oil lamps scattered about on board the ship. However, even with the lamps lit, the darkness was overpowering. Every man and woman on board the ship shuddered within their skin. Not because they feared the dark but because of what might be hiding in it.

Not only was the night as black as the depths of the sea, but it was unnervingly quiet. The ocean was so still they couldn't even hear it lap against the ship's hull. Raven searched for the horizon with her spyglass but couldn't find it. Even with every lamp on the ship lit, the darkness prevailed, making walking from station to station difficult.

Raven gripped the ship's railing, her knuckles white as the oppressive darkness wrapped around them like a shroud. The silence was deafening. No wind stirred the sails. The ocean was as smooth as black glass, stretching forever in every direction.

Then, she heard it.

A soft, rhythmic sound—waves lapping against the hull. But how? The sea was still, and there was no breeze to push them forward. Yet, as she peered over the side, a slow, deliberate motion tugged the ship ahead as if unseen hands beneath the surface guided them deeper into the unknown.

"Raven?" Attila's voice wavered. "The ship is moving."

"I know," Raven murmured, her pulse quickening. "But there's no wind, no current...nothing."

A murmur of unease rippled through the crew. Boots shuffled against the deck as Raven's crew rushed to check the sails, the helm, and anything that might explain what was happening. But there was nothing. No rational reason why their ship should be drifting forward, steady and slow, toward whatever lay beyond the darkness.

A deep, unnatural chill settled in Raven's bones. She turned to John, whose face had gone pale beneath the dim lantern light. "Ever seen anything like this before?"

John hesitated, then shook his head. "Not in any sea I'd want to sail."

A shiver ran down Raven's spine as she gripped the hilt of her sword. They weren't just moving blindly through the void—something was leading them. And she had the sinking feeling that it wasn't by choice wherever they were going.

Everyone held onto the nearest rail or rigging to support themselves as *Destiny* rolled through the still waters under some invisible power. She began slowly, but as she moved along, her speed increased. Faster and faster, *Destiny* rolled along. The ship's rigging moaned at the force being placed upon it as the sails moved against the force. Raven feared the rigging and sails might be torn to shreds if they didn't furl the sails.

"Jeremy! Furl the sails before they are torn apart!"

"Aye, Raven!"

Jeremy sent his crew into action, climbing up the rigging and working earnestly against the invisible force taxing their sails. The men struggled to hold themselves up on the crosstrees while trying to roll the sails back up. As each sail was rolled, the ship's speed increased.

Raven stood on the quarterdeck, holding onto the port rail as the ship's speed increased. Her cheeks felt like they were being pulled away from her face by the force of the wind. She guessed their speed to be at least forty or fifty knots. The fastest she had ever traveled in the sea was twelve or thirteen knots. Raven's stomach churned, and her eyes watered from the cold, quick wind that blew against her face.

Isaac stood at the helm, trying to keep Destiny steered straight, but it was no use. The wheel seemed to have a mind of its own, and Isaac couldn't budge it even a quarter of a turn. Once the sails were rolled up, the crew climbed back to the main deck and held on for dear life.

Raven noticed that even as fast as they were traveling through the water, the ship wasn't bouncing as she would have expected. A ship sailing through a storm or even calmer seas would canter between the waves. Theirs wasn't the case. It was as if they were gliding on solid, level ground. Their speed continued to increase the farther along they traveled. The sky was still black. Nothing could be seen in the distance. If not for the light of their lanterns, the men would be completely blind.

Then, a small glimpse of light appeared in the distance in the direction they traveled. Muziki stood at the ship's bow and noticed it first.

"Ahoy, Raven! I think I see a light up ahead!"

Raven took out her spyglass and pointed it in the direction Muziki was pointing. Through her lens, she spotted a dark blue light mixed with shades of purple. The light grew as Destiny approached it. Raven realized the light wasn't growing; they were moving closer to it. Raven tucked her spyglass into her satchel and ordered her men, "Everyone get below decks and batten down the hatches. We can't do anything about controlling the ship, so secure yourselves in your bunks."

The light was changing as everyone moved below decks. Raven saw that it wasn't just a light; there was a black opening in the horizon where the blue and purple light swirled around it. It appeared to be a tunnel of some sort. The blue was circling the black clockwise. The ship was now moving at least fifty or sixty knots.

"Hurry!" she yelled at everyone as she ran to her cabin, slammed the door, and secured the hatch behind her.

When Raven locked her door, the room tossed her over as the ship spun into the blue vortex. Her table and stools overturned as all her charts and nautical instruments spilled onto the floor. Raven was slammed into the wall of her cabin, hitting her head on the cabinet that hung on the wall, knocking her unconscious.

Her frightened little monkey, Captain Billings, bounced over to check on her and screeched when Raven didn't awaken.

CHAPTER 26

Raven heard muffled voices.

Someone was running past her cabin out on the main deck. Someone else was barking orders. She couldn't tell what they were saying. Raven raised her hand to the side of her head and found it wrapped in a bandage. Her head was throbbing. She tried to raise herself, but the room began to spin, so she lay back down. Then, she heard a familiar voice.

"Ah! You're awake."

It was Andrew Greer.

The fog in her head began to clear, bit by bit.

"Where is Papa? Is he alright?"

"Aye, Raven. He's up on the quarterdeck running things for you."

Raven looked around the room and saw that everything seemed to be in place.

"Who put my room back in place?"

"What do you mean, dear?"

"The room tumbled when we went through the blue vortex."

"The blue what?"

"How long have I been asleep?"

"Oh, you've been out for five days now."

Raven asked, "Where are we?"

"We're going to Ireland to drop Mr. O'Toole off."

"Did the repairs work? Did you get the new rudder installed?"

Greer looked at his captain with a look of concern.

"Rest here, child. I'll go and get Mr. Ashworth for you."

Raven closed her eyes and wished her head would stop throbbing. She felt a familiar tug on her hair. Captain Billings squeaked and stroked her hair. Raven reached up to find him with her hand and found his tiny head. She rubbed his tiny ear. Petting the monkey seemed to relieve the pain in her head.

John bounded through the doorway and ran to his daughter's bedside.

"Raven? Are you alright, daughter?"

"Yes, Papa. I think I'm fine."

Raven tried once more to raise herself in her bed. John helped and supported her as she swung her legs off the bed, letting her bare feet hang over the side.

"How's that?" John asked.

"That's fine. I'm still a little dizzy, but my head doesn't hurt quite as much."

Raven sat befuddled for a moment, thinking of what she last remembered. She remembered being tossed about by the churning vortex before hitting her head. Before that, she remembered the island that had held them captive. She remembered all the strange creatures on the island: the dinosaurs, the ape-like men, the giant ants.

Then, she remembered the loss of so many of her men. *Jeffrey*. She teared up and began to weep uncontrollably.

"What is it, Raven?"

"Oh, Papa, I shall never see him again. I've lost him."

"Who?"

She sniffed as she looked into his eyes, "Jeffrey."

As she continued to cry, her father comforted her and said, "Raven, Jeffrey is fine."

"No, he isn't. He fell into the quicksand. He's dead."

"Raven, there is no quicksand. We've been at sea for five days now. Jeffrey is up on the quarterdeck with Jeremy and Mdago."

"Mdago was killed too. A huge lion with extra-long teeth attacked him. An...and Bila Meno was killed and eaten by the ape-men. Giant ants ate Seremala."

"No, daughter. It must have been a dream. All of those you just spoke of are on this ship, alive and well."

Raven brushed away her tears and asked, "Really?"

"Yes, really. Let me go and find Jeffrey for you."

John left her room and went to the quarterdeck to find Jeffrey.

Raven sat alone at the edge of her bed, still trying to overcome her brain fog and understand everything that had happened to her. Or did it?"

A knock came to her door, and Raven said, "Come in."

The door opened, and there stood the handsome young man with whom Raven suddenly realized she was in love with.

"Jeffrey!"

She tried to walk to him but faltered. Jeffery caught her before she fell, held her in his arms, and kissed her. Raven sobbed as he held her. Her joy of not having lost him was overwhelming. She pulled her lips away from him and buried her face in his chest as she continued to weep. Jeffery was content to hold her for a time.

"Oh, Jeffrey, I thought I had lost you."

"What? What are you talking about?"

Raven explained, "I guess it was a dream, no, a nightmare. But it seemed so real yet unbelievable. *Destiny* was taken by storm to a mysterious island where everything was wrong. We met three men there who were from the future. They were soldiers, I think. Anyway, everything on the island was strange. The plants were too large, and they shot out poison darts that would put you to sleep if you touched them. There were ants the size of large dogs and hairless dogs the size of horses. There were men covered with hair from head to toe who captured Bila Meno and ate him."

"What?"

"Yes, and large lions with long teeth protruding from their mouths like elephant tusks. One of them killed Mdago. And there were these things called dinosaurs that were like giant lizards. Oh, and dragons."

"Wow! Sounds like quite the dream."

Raven continued. "And you. You fell into quicksand, and I tried to save you but couldn't. You sank, and I couldn't get to you." Raven began to sob again. "I tried."

Jeffrey held her close again and tried to comfort her.

"It's alright. You're alright. I'm here with you, and you're safe."

"I know, but it was so real."

Raven pushed away and looked into Jeffrey's eyes. "I want to tell you something."

"What is it?"

She paused before speaking.

"I promised myself if somehow we returned to each other, I would tell you something."

"What is it?"

"Jeffrey, I love you. I think I always have. I don't know why I haven't told you before, but I'm telling you... "

Jeffery pulled her close and kissed her again. A kiss that lasted seemingly forever.

Two days later, Raven joined John and Jeffrey on the quarterdeck as they sailed northward toward Ireland. Raven held onto the rail at the front of the deck to keep her balance because she was still unsteady after her head injury.

It did her men good to see their captain on deck again. She had been confined to her quarters for what felt like a long time, even though it was only about a week. The men sang their songs as they labored on deck.

"Tutafanya Kazi asubuki!"
  (*We will work in the morning*)
  Crew: "Fanya Kazi kill situ!"
  (*Work every day*)
  Leader: " Tutafanya Kazi Mchana kutwa!"
  (*We will work in the daytime*)
  Crew: "Fanya Kazi kill situ!"
  (*Work every day*)
  Leader: "Tutafanya Kazi zote hadi mwezi utakapokuja!"
  (*We will work until the moon comes*)
  Crew: "Fanya Kazi kill situ!"
  (*Work every day*)

Raven felt joy as she heard them sing. It seemed like the perfect day—no more worries about dinosaurs, dragons, sea monsters, or ape-men.

She soon spotted Sean O'Toole walking along the deck. He looked up and noticed Raven was finally out of her cabin and standing on the quarterdeck. Sean waved to her, and she nodded. He walked over to the quarterdeck but didn't climb up. Instead, he stood below the rail, looking up at her, and conversed.

"Aye, lassie. It's so good to see you up and about once again. How're ya feelin' then?"

"Much better, Mr. O'Toole."

"Oh, well, that's fine then. Would ya be interested in havin' a wee bit of a drink wit me later on?"

Raven smiled, "Why don't you have supper with me tonight? We can toast to your return home."

"That sounds lovely, lass. I'll be seein' ya then."

Sean turned and walked away, continuing his stroll around the ship's main deck. Raven noticed a group of small islands on the ship's starboard side and asked Attila to give her their location.

"Raven, we are about five hundred miles off the coast of Morocco."

"Are those the Canary Islands, then?"

"Aye, Raven. They are."

"We should be about halfway to Dublin then?"

"Aye. If the wind holds up, we should be there in six or seven days."

Jeffrey entered the galley and found Louis Hardy at his usual post, cleaning and chopping vegetables for the evening meal.

"Oh, hello, Mr. Hamilton. Is there something you be needing?"

"Aye, Mr. Hardy. I was wondering if you could prepare something special for tonight's evening meal. Raven will be having guests, and it will be a special occasion."

"Special occasion, sir?"

"Well, you know, since she is feeling better."

"I see, yes. How many guests will there be?"

"Let's see; there's Mr. Ashworth, of course, Mr. O'Toole, Raven, and me, Captain Attila, Hadari, and Jeremy. Yes, I think that will be about it."

"Seven for supper. Right, Mr. Hamilton. I'll fix something special for you all, sir."

"Thank you, Mr. Hardy."

"Think nothing of it, sir. It be my pleasure."

Mr. Hardy sent Kupika below decks to find the two most plump, healthy hens she could find among the brood they had stored below, providing them with eggs. While Kupika went below, Mr. Hardy prepared a large pot of boiling water to scald the hens in after they had been slaughtered. Hardy had to feed the stove a bit to get it hot enough to boil such a large pot of water. When Kupika returned from below, she carried two hens upside down by their feet.

"The water is almost ready. Go ahead and kill the ole girls, then bring them back in for the scalding."

"Aye, Mr. Hardy."

Kupika stepped outside on the main deck, holding the two hens and a hatchet in one hand. She hung one of the hens on a hook at the rail, took the other hen, and laid her on a cutting board on the deck. She skillfully swung the hatchet down, severing the hen's head from her body. As the hen flopped around on deck, Kupika took the other hen from the hook and cut her head off, too. She held both hens over the rail and allowed the blood to drain from their bodies into the ocean. Once the blood flow had decreased to a slow drip, Kupika took them back into the galley to scald them.

When she entered the galley, Kupika saw that the water was now in full rolling boil. She dipped one of the hens into the scalding hot water and held it there for about half a minute. Then she pulled the hen out of the water and did the same with the second. The scalding would allow Kupika to remove the feathers from the hen with little effort. Once both hens were scalded, she took them back onto the deck to begin plucking.

Once all the feathers had been removed, Kupika began dressing out the hens. She first cut off the necks and placed them into a pan. She removed the hens' rectal vents from the flesh by poking her knife into the flesh surrounding the vent and cutting around the vent, separating the intestinal tract from the outer skin of the hens. She reached through the neck opening and began to pull the inner organs from the body cavity. She removed the gizzard, heart, and liver from the hens and placed them in the pan with the necks. She cut off the feet and washed all the parts and the inside and outside of each hen with water before carrying them back into the galley for Mr. Hardy.

Hardy looked the hens over as they lay in the pan and remarked, "Oh, that's a fine job now, Kupika. They will make a lovely meal for Mr. Hamilton's party tonight."

"Thank you, Mr. Hardy."

Louis put the hens on a spit and set them to roast in the open fire pit above the fire. He had Kupika wash and prepare potatoes and carrots to be roasted in the oven while he peeled and cut up various fruits to accompany the hens.

Once Hardy had finished the side dishes, he made a bread pudding to be served for dessert.

Portree
SCOT
Stirli
Glasgow
NORTHERN
IRELAND
Sligo
Isle of
Dundalk
Drogheda
Dublin
Galway
Ireland
Limerick
Kilkenny
Tralee
Waterford
Dingle
Killarney
WA
Cork

CHAPTER 27

Raven was surprised to see everyone as they filed into her cabin at mealtime. She looked at Jeffrey and asked, "Did I miss something? I don't recall planning a party tonight."

"I hope you don't mind. I thought it might be nice to have a little celebration since you have finally overcome your injury and awakened."

"Not at all. Is there anyone else joining us tonight?"

"It will be just the seven of us tonight. Mr. Hardy has prepared a special meal for us all."

"Wonderful! I can't wait to see what Hardy has prepared."

A knock came at the door, and Jeremy opened it. There stood Louis Hardy and Kupika carrying the night's supper. Louis carried a large tray holding the two roasted hens surrounded by the roasted vegetables. Kupika carried a second tray holding the bread pudding surrounded by the cut fruit. They each set their trays on the table before the party and listened as Raven and her guests complimented them for the excellent-smelling dishes they had prepared. Kupika began pouring wine into each person's glass. Once everyone was served, Mr. Hardy and Kupika exited the captain's quarters to continue their duties in the galley.

Raven remarked, "My, it looks so delicious. It seems like ages since I feasted like this."

Jeffrey replied, "Well, you have been asleep for some time. I thought it was time for you to regain your strength and celebrate your recovery."

"Thank you, Jeffrey."

Jeffrey looked into Raven's eyes and smiled as she thanked him for the gesture.

Everyone served themselves as the platters were passed around the table. Everything was delicious. However, Raven could only nibble at the food on her plate. Although she hadn't eaten in almost a week, she had little appetite. She nibbled on a bite or two of the chicken and some of the fruit. The bread pudding looked terrific, but she couldn't bring herself to eat any.

When everyone had finished eating and was content with sipping their wine, Jeffrey stood to get their attention.

"Thank you, everyone, for joining us this evening as we celebrate the return of our fair captain. Raven, we're delighted you have overcome your injuries."

Jeffrey stepped over to Raven and took her by the hand to raise her from her seat.

"I am delighted you have recovered from your head injury and can lead us all again. Dear Raven, you mean more to me than I can ever express."

Jeffery knelt before Raven, holding her hand, saying, "Raven, I love you more than life itself. I can't imagine living here on this earth without you. Would you do me the honor of becoming my wife?"

Jeffrey took a ring from his vest pocket and presented it to Raven. It was a gold ring encrusted with seven small diamonds and seven rubies. Raven gasped when she saw the ring. She had never allowed herself to think about marriage. She was too much of a free spirit—an adventurer. She still had so much to accomplish in her life. The high seas were calling her name. Yet, after having experienced the loss of Jeffrey in her dream, she realized there was more to life than sailing across the world. Maybe it was time to settle down and raise a family.

Raven wiped a tear from her eye as she gathered her composure to answer.

She took a deep breath and replied, "Yes, Jeffrey. I will marry you."

Everyone sitting at the table gave a subtle cheer and raised their glasses to the couple, who now embraced and kissed to seal their agreement. John was decidedly excited about the news that his only daughter might present him with grandchildren.

John said, "Wonderful! When can we have the wedding?"

Raven looked at Jeffrey and responded, "Well, I don't know. I've just been asked. We haven't had time to plan anything."

Jeffrey replied, "Right. We have plenty of time. There is no rush. I'm sure you want Pharaoh and Alexander to be present when it happens."

"Absolutely! We should plan on having the ceremony at the Robin's Nest—that way, all of our crew can attend."

Jeffrey replied, "Yes. Maybe we could pick up some items in Dublin to take to the Robin's Nest for our wedding."

"Now that you mention it, a wedding dress might be appropriate. And a new suit for you. My maids will need dresses as well. Who will stand in as your best man?"

"Well, I haven't thought of that yet. I feel close to John, yet he will need to give you away. Maybe one of your captains?"

Attila said, "I would be happy to stand for you, Mr. Hamilton."

"Thank you, Attila. I appreciate it. I would be honored to have you as my best man."

Everyone continued celebrating the news of Jeffrey and Raven's wedding plans. They drank much wine and rum as the night waned. Raven had to ask everyone to excuse her so she could rest. She still felt the effects of her recent head trauma and wanted to sleep.

Everyone left her cabin except Jeffrey, who lingered.

He asked, "Is this really happening? Are we going to be married?"

"It seems so."

Raven smiled as she looked up into his blue eyes and kissed him.

Jeffrey eased his embrace and said, "I'll leave you now so you can rest. See you in the morning?"

"Absolutely."

As Raven stood on the quarterdeck, Mdago called from the crow's nest.

"Land ho! Off the port bow!"

Raven took out her spyglass to search the horizon. The land was barely visible, but it was there. If their charts and navigation were correct, they were looking at the southern tip of Ireland.

Raven ordered, "Steady on. We'll turn 20º starboard when we get closer and head toward Dublin."

John, who stood beside Isaac the helmsman, replied, "Aye, Raven. Steady as she goes."

Every hour brought them closer to the picturesque view of the rolling emerald-colored hills of the Irish countryside.

Sean stood on the bow, looking longingly at his homeland as they sailed closer and closer. He took a deep breath, recognizing the familiar smell of his motherland. He smiled with delight. Raven strolled up to him and asked, "What do you think?"

"Aye, there be no lovelier island in the world, lass. I've missed it so."

"Is Dublin your home?"

"Aye, it tis. Although I dunno if my fam'ly is still here or no."

Raven touched Sean's shoulder and said, "Well, we'll be at port for at least a day while we resupply. You're welcome if you change your mind and want to come with us."

"Aye, lass. I hope it won't come ta that."

When *Destiny* was docked, Sean skipped down the gangplank and waved goodbye to all aboard. He smiled as he skipped through the streets of Dublin, wandering back to his home. Not much had changed in the time he had been gone. However, many of the faces had changed.

Many faces stared as Sean moved down the cobbled streets of the city. They wondered who the old man with the long grey beard and ragged clothing might be. Sean wasn't concerned with their demeaning looks. He was too happy to be back home.

Sean made a right onto a side street called Calabash, twelve blocks from the docks. He walked another two blocks and looked up to find the building he once called home. He stood and admired it for a while before going to the entry door. Sean opened the door and entered. He stood in a small entryway that led to several downstairs apartments and a stairway that led to more apartments on the upper floors.

Sean climbed the steps leading to the third and top floor. At the top, he turned left and found the door to his old flat. He paused a moment before knocking lightly on the door. He heard heavy footsteps coming toward the door. The door opened abruptly, and Sean found himself face-to-face with an older man wearing a scowl.

"Yeah? What duh ya want?"

"Pardon me, sir. I'm looking for Mary O'Toole. Might ya know her?"

"What might ya want wit Mary?"

"I'm Sean O'Toole. I'm her husband."

The man's eyes widened with surprise.

"We thought ye be dead."

"Is she here then?"

"Aye, she be here. MARY!"

A frail woman came from the back of the flat toward the door, wiping her hands on her apron.

"What tis it, Brady?"

When she looked up and saw the strange man standing at the door, she asked, "Who tis it?"

"Mary? tis me. Sean...your husband."

Mary's brow furrowed as she stood looking at the man at her door. "Sean? Sean O'Toole? I thought ya be dead. Where ya been all dese years?"

"I were shipwrecked on an island in the Caribbean, living with a bunch of savages. I've only now been rescued and brought back to Ireland. Where are duh children?"

"Children? Sean, Gladys died a year after ya left...and Seamus is a growed-up man and married. He and his bride moved to the Americas."

"Seamus, married? He's only a lad."

"What ya be talking about, Sean? He's twenty year old."

"Twenty? How long have I been gone, den?"

"Sean, it's been more dan ten year. I've moved on. This is my husband, Brady."

"Your husband, say you? But, Mary, I come back to ya."

"Did ya 'spect me to wait fer ya forever, now? If it hadn't been for Brady here, we'd been kicked to duh streets long ago."

Tears rolled down Sean's cheeks, "But Mary. What am I ta do?"

"I dunno. But do it somewheres else."

Mary slammed the door in Sean's face.

Sean turned and walked back down the staircase until he found the door leading back to the street. He sighed as he turned the latch and opened the door. He didn't know what to do or where to go. He walked along the cobblestones, heading back to the docks. Sean never looked up, but he could feel the stares of those who watched him move through the city. A stranger in their midst. Unwashed, wearing rags and an unkempt hair and beard.

Sean found himself standing back at the gangplank leading up to *Raven's Destiny*. He looked up and saw Raven looking at him at the top of the gangplank. Raven knew he was distraught.

"Come aboard, Sean."

Sean walked up the gangplank until he was standing before Raven.

"Did you find your family?"

Sean shook his head. "They're all gone."

"Dead?"

"As good as. My daughter is dead. My son moved to the Americas, and Mary had fount another man tuh take me place."

"I'm sorry to hear that, Sean. Any idea what you're going to do?"

"I dunno."

"Come with us. I can always use another man on my crew."

Sean's face brightened with the offer. "Really?"

"Aye. But we need to get you properly fitted. Come along. We need to find a shop with some proper clothing for you. And maybe a barber, too."

Sean followed Raven down the gangplank back to the docks. As they reached the docks, a dirty, rag-wearing boy approached Raven.

"Pardon me, miss. Is the captain onboard?"

"No, you're looking at the captain."

"You miss? You're duh captain?"

"Aye, the name's Captain Raven Ashworth. And this is *Raven's Destiny*. What can I do for you?"

"Please, Captain. I'm looking for work onboard a ship."

Raven looked the boy over and asked, "Where are your parents?"

"Me ma and da are dead, miss."

"How?"

"Ma died of fever, and robbers killed da. I've been alone since I was ten."

"How old are you now?"

"Twelve, Captain."

Raven examined the boy before asking, "What's your name?"

"Michael. Michael Murphy."

"Well, Michael Murphy, I started working on a ship when I was twelve. How would you like to be my new ship's boy?"

Michael's eyes lit up as he replied, "Aye, Captain!"

"Alright then. Come along. We'll clean you up and get you properly outfitted before we cast off."

Chapter 28

Raven and her two companions walked through the streets, first looking for a bathhouse with a barbershop. As they walked along the cobblestones, Raven noticed a sign up ahead that read, "Barber-Surgeon."

"Here we are," she said.

As they stepped inside, they saw four barber chairs in the front room. The proprietor, a short, heavy man with an almost bald head, greeted them.

"Good day, me, lady... gents. What can I do for yuhs?"

Raven replied, "These two gentlemen need a bath and haircut, and Sean needs a shave, too."

"Right then. My name is Alister Barber, and I can meet all your needs."

Raven asked, "Barber? Really?"

"Aye, miss. My family were barbers for as long as I can trace them back. Back when people got their names from whatever their trade or occupation might be."

"Fascinating," Raven said.

Mr. Barber looked at the two and asked, "Would yuh like their garments washed too?"

"No, that won't be necessary. We will, however, need new clothing for them. Preferably garments suitable for working men."

"Right, yuh are, miss. O'Reilly's just up the street and on the right will be what yuh be looking for. They can supply whatever yuh need."

"Thank you, Mr. Barber."

Raven paid the barber for his services before leaving the shop to find O'Reilly's. Mr. Barber showed Michael and Sean to the back room where the baths were set up. Fresh water was being warmed in a large cauldron over an open fire. Four copper tubs were lined up along the back wall. Water was already in each tub, most likely already used by previous customers. Sean disrobed and climbed into the nearest tub to the fire. Michael chose the last tub, hoping for a little more privacy.

Mr. Barber brought each of them a clean towel and a bar of soap. Using a wooden bucket, he dipped hot water from the caldron and poured it into each tub to warm the water. The water felt good to their bones as they closed their eyes and soaked in the clean feeling of the hot bath. Sean took his soap and scrubbed his body from head to toe. Michael watched from a distance and mimicked the older man. Michael had not had a bath in at least two years and was unfamiliar with the process.

After they had lathered themselves, Mr. Barber brought over another bucket of warm water and poured it over each patron's head to rinse away the soap. Michael made the mistake of breathing while the bucket was poured over his head, and he began to choke and cough.

Raven entered O'Reilly's and was greeted by a bell ringing above the door.

Timothy O'Reilly was a man of about forty, skinny and tall, almost six feet. He wore a grey wool suit and black leather shoes.

"May I help you, miss?"

Raven replied, "Yes, please. I have two men I have just hired to work on my ship who need new work clothes."

Timothy asked, "Do you know their measurements?"

"No. I can estimate their size, but they are now bathing at Mr. Barber's."

"Oh, well, that will be no problem. Why don't I go down and get their measurements so we can find whatever they need?"

"Sounds wonderful."

"Elizabeth?" Timothy called to the back room.

A woman with bright red hair, very much like Raven's, came from the back.

"Would you please watch the front while I go down to Mr. Barber's for some measurements?"

"Of course, Dear."

Timothy picked up a pad, a pencil, and a measuring tape, then escorted Raven back to the Barbershop. When they arrived at the barbershop, Raven found Sean sitting in the barber's chair, wrapped in two towels—one draped over his shoulders and chest, the other covering his lower extremities. Michael was sitting in a chair against the wall, dressed similarly, waiting for his turn.

Raven motioned for Michael to stand so Timothy could take his measurements. The young man stood with his arms outstretched and waiting as the tailor measured him from head to toe and fingertips. By the time O'Reilly finished with Michael, Sean was finished in the barber's chair, so they traded places.

Raven almost didn't recognize Sean. "My, how different you look!"

Sean was clean-shaven, and his hair was cropped short. "I feel like me old self. Or maybe I should say, me younger self."

Timothy measured Sean, then proceeded to his shop to find the proper garments Raven's men would need. Raven walked along with him to pay for the clothing. As soon as they walked into the shop, Timothy went straight to the shelves and began selecting various trousers, shirts, stockings, shoes, undergarments, and cold-weather gear.

"Will there be anything else?"

Raven replied, "No, thank you. I think that should be enough to get them at least started."

Timothy added up the amount owed and finished Raven's transaction.

"Would you like me to help you carry these back to the barbershop?"

"If you wouldn't mind."

"Absolutely, it would be my pleasure."

Elizabeth looked sideways at her husband as he interacted with the beautiful young pirate.

Timothy turned and said, "I'll only be a moment, dear." Then he noticed the look on Elizabeth's face. He cleared his throat uncomfortably as he turned to walk away.

Raven and Timothy returned to the barbershop carrying the clothing for her new crew members. When they entered the shop, she found Sean and Michael still wrapped in their towels.

"Here you are," she said, handing Michael his new outfit.

Michael stared at the clothes in awe. He had never owned anything new before. All of his clothing had belonged to someone else before he wore it.

"Thank you, Captain!"

Michael ran to the back room to dress. Sean collected his new clothes from Mr. O'Reilly and also disappeared into the back room. When they returned to the front room, Raven and Timothy examined them to ensure all the garments fit just right. Once satisfied, O'Reilly returned to his shop after receiving payment from Raven.

Raven said to her new men, "Well now, I think it's time we got onboard the ship and cast off. What say you?"

Michael gave an enthusiastic, "Aye, Captain!"

Sean smiled and followed Raven and the boy out the door and down the cobblestone street back to the docks.

As Raven walked up the gangplank, she was met by Jeremy at the rail.

"Jeremy, have all the supplies been loaded?"

"Aye, Raven. We're all set and ready to launch."

"Very good. Prepare to cast off."

"Aye, Raven."

"Oh, and Jeremy, put these two to work. You know Sean, and this is Michael Murphy, our new ship's boy."

Jeremy looked at them both. Then he looked intently at Sean. "Mr. O'Toole?"

"Aye, Mr. Finch, at your service, I be."

"I didn't recognize you."

"Well now, I hardly recognized me self."

Jeremy turned his attention to the rest of the crew and ordered, "Cast off the bow line!"

As the ship drifted from the dock, Jeremy ordered, "Cast off the stern!"

Jeremy turned to the new men and said, "Mr. O'Toole, please join the crew as they prepare to unfurl the sails. Mr. Murphy, follow me, and I'll introduce you to Mr. Greer."

They both replied in unison, "Aye, Mr. Finch."

Michael followed Jeremy as he led the way past the galley to the infirmary to find Mr. Greer.

"It wasn't so long ago I was a ship's boy, you know."

"Really? How old were you when you started, sir?"

" I was thirteen years old."

"And may I ask, sir, how old are you now?"

"I'm sixteen."

"Blimey! Only sixteen and running the ship?"

Michael noticed the men as they worked the rigging, preparing to unfurl the sails.

"May I ask, sir, how many slaves are onboard?"

Jeremy stopped and turned to the boy.

"There are no slaves aboard this ship or any of Raven's ships. All these men are free. Raven freed every one of them. We are all loyal to Raven all the way to the end. And she is loyal to us. There's no one tougher or more capable of sailing the high seas as The Red Raven."

"The Red Raven, sir?"

"That's how she is known, and known she is. There's not a sailing vessel anywhere in the Atlantic or the Caribbean that hasn't heard of The Red Raven."

Jeremy looked down at the boy and said, "I bet she bought you those new clothes, didn't she?"

"Yes, sir."

"That's the kind of person she is. Generous to her men. But those who cross her will find themselves at the point of her blade. So make sure you don't cross her."

"Blimey, no, sir."

Jeremy continued the tour past the galley and pointed out Mr. Hardy, the ship's cook. They entered the infirmary, where they found Mr. Greer.

"Mr. Greer, this is our new ship's boy, Michael Murphy."

"Ah, Mr. Murphy. Welcome aboard."

"Thank you, sir."

Jeremy excused himself from the two, saying, "Mr. Greer, I'll leave him in your capable hands."

"Aye, Mr. Finch."

Raven stood on the quarterdeck, watching Sean as he made his first climb up the rigging to the cross tree of the mainsail. He stumbled through the climb a bit, trying to get his sea legs, but soon recovered and finished his climb to help unfurl the mainsail.

The sun was already lowering at her right shoulder as *Destiny* drifted southward through the bay. Jeffrey stepped up next to Raven as they watched the men work the rigging to get underway. Jeremy gave the order to unfurl the mainsail, and the men standing on the cross tree untied the lashes holding the sail in place. The sheet dropped and billowed out, caught by a steady tailwind, sending the ship into a ten-knot glide through the water. As each of the sails was unfurled, the ship's speed increased, carrying *Destiny* out of the bay, traveling at twelve knots.

Twenty-four hours after they began their journey back to the Robin's Nest, Raven changed course as they reached the mouth of the English Channel. Raven wanted to evade the coast of France at all costs. She knew the French navy was still looking for her, and she didn't want to make it any easier for them by sailing right past their naval headquarters. She had Isaac turn West by Southwest to avoid the French coastline.

Raven called up to Mdago, who was manning the crow's nest, "Mdago, keep a sharp eye out for any French flags sailing about!"

"Aye, Raven!"

Mdago scanned the horizon with his spyglass, searching for any ships in the area, especially those flying France's blue, white, and red stripes. Once they had reached a point 400 miles off the Westernmost coast of France, Raven directed Isaac Finch to turn South.

All seemed clear along the French coast. No ships were spotted anywhere toward *Destiny's* port side. However, 170 miles due Northwest of Spain and 450 miles due West of France, Mdago spotted a ship coming from the West.

"Ship ahoy off the starboard side!"

Raven pulled out her spyglass and looked. From her location on the quarterdeck, she couldn't spot a ship.

"Can you make out its colors?"

Mdago looked again and replied, "Not yet!"

Raven nervously waited for Mdago to update her on the approaching ship's status. Sweat began to trickle down her brow toward her nose. She wiped it away.

A call from the crow's nest announced, "It's a French frigate! It's heading straight for us!"

Raven turned to John, who was standing next to her. John asked, "Do we fight?"

Raven's mind raced, searching for the correct answer.

"No. Strike the colors and hoist the British flag. We're an English merchant ship leaving Dublin heading to Argentina to pick up a load of cashews. You're captain now."

John nodded his understanding.

"Where will you be?"

"I'll be hiding under my bed like a frightened little girl."

As Raven fled to her quarters, John took over as the ship's captain.

"Mr. Finch! Strike the colors and hoist the British flag. We are now a merchant ship."

"Aye, Mr. Ashworth!"

"Attention, crew! If we should be boarded, we are a British merchant ship leaving Dublin heading for Argentina. I am Captain John Crane. Understood?"

"Aye, Captain Crane!" they all responded.

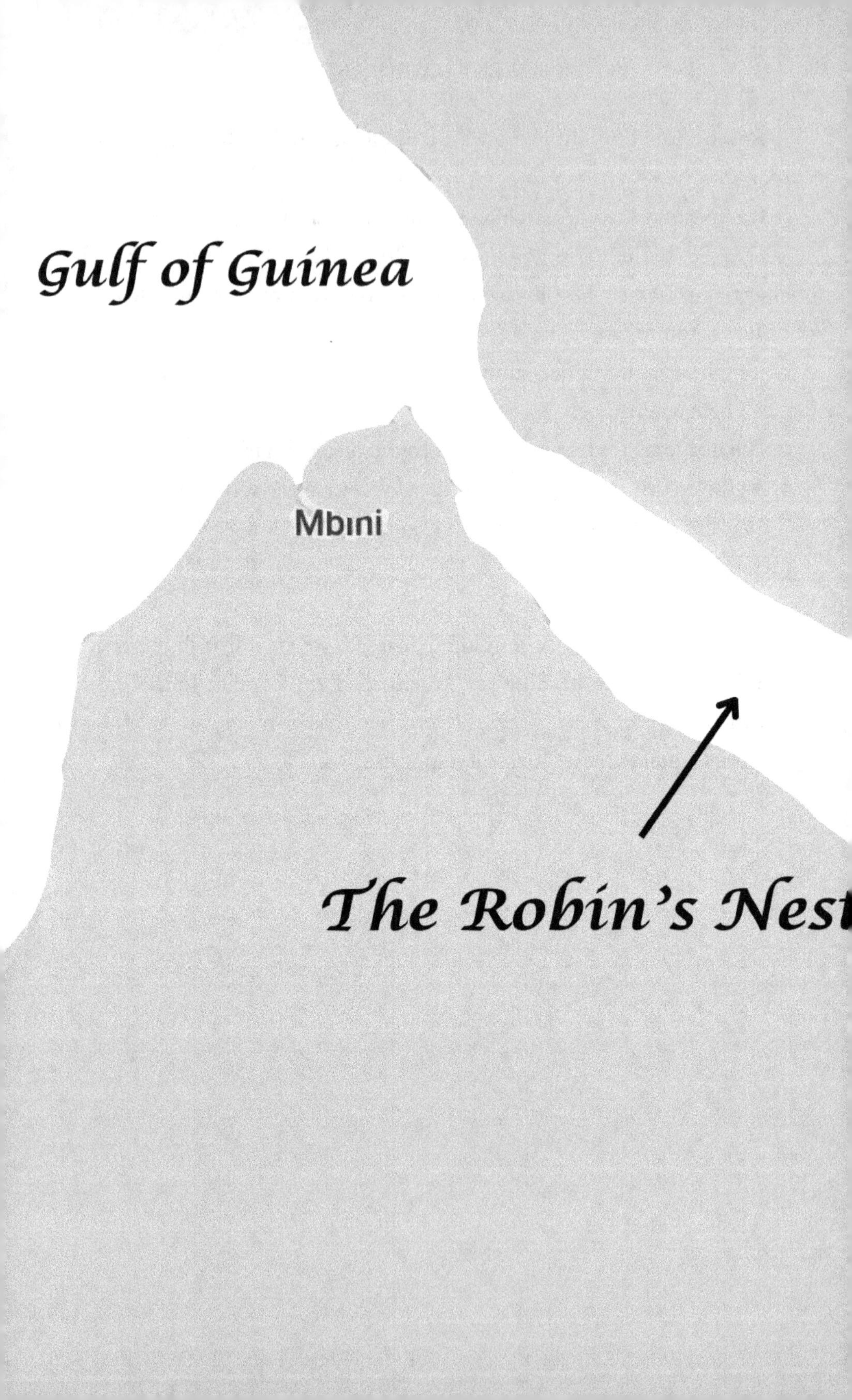

Gulf of Guinea
Mbini
The Robin's Nest

CHAPTER 29

Raven hastened to leave the quarterdeck before she might be spotted by the frigate. As she returned to her cabin, she called Michael to join her. Michael quickly followed her to her quarters and waited for instructions. Raven entered her cabin and immediately cleared anything from sight, indicating a woman was onboard the vessel. Michael looked around the cabin, taking in all the instruments and charts displayed throughout the room. Raven raised the mattress on her bed and began stuffing the hidden compartment beneath with all her belongings that might reveal her gender, including her jade gown. Michael was a bit confused by her actions but stood by, waiting for instructions.

"Michael, this is very important. You have never seen me. You don't know who I am. Do you understand?"

"Aye, Captain."

"Mr. Ashworth is your captain now. Only his name is Captain Crane."

"I understand."

"I need you to take Captain Billings with you and keep him safe. Don't bring him back in here until it is safe."

"Captain Billings, Captain?"

Raven pointed to the monkey curled up on a shelf at the corner of the room.

"Does he bite?"

"Not if he likes you. Treat him well, and he will be a good friend to you."

"Aye, Captain."

Raven climbed into the hidden compartment beneath her mattress and said, "Put the mattress back in place after I close the lid. Then get moving."

Michael straightened the mattress after Raven closed the lid, then took the monkey back to the main deck and climbed to the quarterdeck to await instructions.

Raven fastened a latch inside the compartment so that anyone searching would think a solid bed frame had been built with no storage beneath. Considering her cramped space, she settled in and made herself as comfortable as possible.

John called Jeremy to the quarterdeck. "Can you load the starboard guns without being obvious about it?"

"Aye. I'll make it look like we are cleaning them for storage. Then cover them with canvas as if we are protecting them from the sea's spray."

"Good, lad. See to it."

Jeremy had his gun crew set up the guns on the starboard side with shot and powder. Instead of setting them against the rail in the firing position, they left the cannons in the recoil position and covered them with canvas.

Jeremy passed from man to man, instructing them to hide arms throughout the ship if needed. They hid swords, knives, and pistols in various locations throughout the ship. Many were hidden in buckets covered in cleaning rags. Others were concealed underneath canvas, folded up in various locations along the main deck. Each man busied himself, doing nothing but watching for the signal to attack if it should come. They polished brass fixtures that didn't need polishing. They swept decks that were clean. They mended sails without holes.

Suddenly, a shot was heard from the approaching ship. John and his men watched as a cannonball whizzed over their bow, indicating they should halt.

John ordered his men, "Prepare to be boarded! Furl those sails and cover up the blood sails so these bloody French won't see them."

It took almost half an hour for the frigate to come alongside *Destiny* in a position where they could board her. As the French vessel approached close enough, its sailors threw grappling hooks over to *Destiny* so the two ships could be pulled and secured together.

Twenty French marines climbed over the side and onto *Destiny*, followed by two officers—a captain and his lieutenant. The marines spread throughout the ship's deck while others remained onboard the frigate and held John's crew at gunpoint.

John approached the captain and asked in his pretentious cockney accent. "Welcome aboard, Captain. What might it be we can help ye with?"

The French captain didn't speak English, but his lieutenant did.

"Monsieur Capitaine, allow me to present Capitaine Michaud Henri de Gaulle of his majesty's Navy. He wishes to know who you are and what you are doing in these waters."

"I am Captain John Crane from Bristol, England, and we are going from Dublin to Argentina to sell and trade goods. We be carrying good Irish whiskey that we just picked up and we plan to trade with those Portuguese savages down there for cotton and cashews."

"Why are there so many Africans aboard your ship?"

"They be cheaper help than trying to find some English blokes to carry the load onboard these merchant ships."

"My men will conduct a search of your ship to make sure it is just as you say. If we find that you are indeed as you claim, you will be allowed to proceed."

"Search away, Leftenant. We got nothing to hide here."

The lieutenant signaled for his marines to search the vessel. They opened hatches, searching for anything out of the ordinary. They made a mess of things, overturning barrels and kicking over anything in their way. Two marines entered the officers' quarters, the galley, and the infirmary and upended everything they could out of spite rather than hoping to find anything. Two others entered the area below the quarterdeck where Raven's quarters were. They tossed the captain's quarters, upending tables, chairs, and shelves. They threw charts onto the floor and scattered them. They upended the mattress to look underneath but found nothing.

Below decks, they still found nothing that seemed peculiar to the marines. As they reported back to the lieutenant, he discovered something was missing.

"Capitaine, you say you are transporting Irish whiskey, yet my men have found none aboard your ship."

"Really? That can't be! I saw the men load it me self only yesterday. Well, I'll get to the bottom of this, I will. Heads are gonna roll, I says."

John turned to Jeremy and nodded.

Jeremy ordered, "Fire!"

Four cannons from the starboard side fired into the frigate's hull in unison at a point-blank position. Men screamed and cursed as the ship's hull exploded into pieces. Shards of timber flew through the air, implanting themselves into the sailors and marines who remained on the frigate.

The captain and lieutenant were shocked by the sudden attack but were suddenly overwhelmed by John's men, who pulled out their weapons from hiding and joined the attack. John pulled out a long knife from the back of his waistband and slit the captain's throat. Attila did the same with the lieutenant. Four of Jeremy's crew broke out swords and hacked the grappling lines to free the two ships from each other.

Gunshots were fired from the frigate, one hitting Jeremy in the right shoulder. He winced in pain but transferred his sword into his left hand and continued to slash at the attacking marines. He thrust his blade into the gut of the nearest marine and pivoted with a quick left turn, slashing at the neck of another marine, nearly decapitating him.

The captain and lieutenant were thrown overboard into the sea, their blood mixing with the salt water. Sharks didn't take long to find their bodies and begin feasting on them.

Destiny's cannons continued to fire into the frigate's hull as the two ships drifted away from one another. Each marine who had boarded *Destiny* was tossed over the side into the drink. Some were already dead. Those who weren't dead fell prey to the frenzy of the sharks.

The frigate began to sink as the open hull began to fill with seawater.

John ordered, "Hoist the sails! Get us out of here before more French dogs come along."

John called out, "Michael!"

Michael came out from his hiding place behind one of the tarps at the ship's bow. John beckoned him to the quarterdeck.

"Michael, return and let Raven know all is safe now."

"Aye, Mr. John."

Michael ran to Raven's quarters and knocked on the side of the bed frame to signal that all was well. She released the latch that locked her hiding place shut and raised the lid to climb out.

"What happened?" she asked.

"I'm not sure. I hid myself and didn't see what happened."

Captain Billings leaped from Michael's shoulder onto Raven's and chirped nervously into her ear. She stroked the monkey's head, trying to soothe him.

"Let's go."

With Captain Billings on her shoulder, Raven led the way as she and Michael returned to the quarterdeck to join John and Attila.

"What happened?"

John replied, "About twenty of them came aboard and searched the ship to verify whether or not we were who we said we were."

"Yes, I could hear them rummaging around in my cabin."

"Well, they discovered we didn't have the cargo we said we were carrying, so they thought they would take us by surprise, but we beat them to it. We blew several holes in the hull, sank the ship, and killed everyone in the process."

"No one was left alive?"

"Sharks got anyone who we didn't kill."

"Very well. Let's get back to the Robin's Nest. I've got a wedding to plan."

Raven's Destiny arrived at the Robin's Nest on a beautiful spring morning soon after sunrise. Raven rose early and stood at the bow as they pulled close to the shore and anchored close to the *Sea Witch*. As they drifted closer to the *Sea Witch*, Raven spotted Pharaoh standing on the quarter-deck, watching as *Destiny* approached. Raven waved.

Pharaoh called out, "I was beginning to worry. What has taken you so long, Raven?"

"Oh, you know me. I just love to make a dramatic entrance. Is all well with you?"

"Aye. We are bored beyond measure."

Destiny dropped anchor alongside the *Sea Witch*. Raven asked that one of the dories be launched to take her ashore. Pharaoh ordered his boat to take him ashore to meet Raven. When they met on the beach, they embraced as old friends. The tall African's arms swallowed Raven as she fell into his embrace.

"It is so good to see you, Raven. I have missed you."

"I feel the same way, Pharaoh. We have much to discuss now that we are reunited."

"Oh? What should we discuss?"

"Well, for one thing, Jeffrey and I are to be wed."

Pharaoh's face lit up with surprise. "What? The Red Raven is getting married? How can this be?"

Raven smiled as she replied, "I guess it was bound to happen sooner or later. Some things that happened while you and I were apart convinced me it was time."

"Oh? I can't wait to hear this story."

"And you will—but later. There is much to do if I am to be wed. By the way, I was hoping you would perform the ceremony."

"I have never done this. I'm not sure what to do."

"We can discuss it later. But I can't imagine having anyone else do this other than you."

"Ah, if you are sure, then I would be honored."

"Wonderful."

Jeffrey walked up to join the two old friends as they spoke. "Did you tell him?"

"I did, and he has agreed to perform the ceremony."

"Thank you, Pharaoh; I know this means so much to Raven for you to be such an integral part of this union. And, to me as well."

"It is my pleasure."

The three friends walked across the beach and into the jungle to select the perfect site for the wedding. Raven remembered a spot nearby she thought would be ideal for her friends and family to gather. She led Pharaoh and Jeffrey to a place about half a mile from the beach where a small waterfall spilled into a freshwater stream leading into the jungle. The spot was surrounded by a grove of mango trees, with a blanket of low-growing grass carpeting the area.

"This is where I want to hold the wedding."

Jeffrey looked the place over and smiled, "How is it I never knew about this place? It's beautiful!"

"A lady has to keep some things to herself. I found it the first time we sailed here, and I have visited it every time we have come here."

"Always alone?"

"Yes. It was my special place where I could contemplate by myself. And now, I want us to share it together."

Chapter 30

The next evening, everyone serving on Raven's two ships gathered at the spot Raven had picked out for the ceremony. It had customarily become known as Raven's Glade. Attila and some of his men constructed an arbor for the bride and groom to stand under during the ceremony. They wove vines and colorful flowers through the thatch work of the arbor to decorate it. The arbor was placed next to the stream, and the waterfall served as a backdrop.

The crews from both ships gathered around on the carpet of grass next to the stream. Pharaoh and Jeffery stood side by side under the arbor, waiting for the bride to arrive. Muziki and his fellow drummers banged out a low-voiced rhythm to signal that the ceremony was beginning. Sean O'Toole held his flute to his lips and began whistling an Irish lullaby along with the rhythm of the drums. The combination of the Irish Celtic tune and the African drum beat was breathtaking.

Alexander escorted Simba, who served as Raven's maid of honor, down the makeshift aisle. She carried a bouquet of island flowers and greenery as she paced toward the arbor. Kupika was next to be led down the aisle by Attila. Finally, John escorted his daughter, Raven, toward the arbor. Raven looked radiant, wearing her jade green gown and a crown of flowers in her hair. Jeffrey gasped as he saw her walking toward him. The crowd was vocal in their approval of their captain's attire. When she reached the arbor where Pharaoh and Jeffrey were waiting, John presented Raven's hand to Jeffrey before stepping aside.

Pharaoh began, "My friends, we are gathered here today to honor and witness the joining of these two in the bonds of marriage."

Pharaoh presented a vine made of flowers that had been woven together. He wrapped the vine around Raven's wrist, then around Jeffrey's, before tying the ends together to make a knot.

"This knot represents a bond which can not be broken. The bond of marriage is to be a commitment for life. Each of you must vow to cling to one another only. Let no one come between you as you live your lives together. Make this commitment to each other a lasting commitment until death breaks the bond. Raven, do you take Jeffrey to be your husband for now and forever?"

Raven looked into Jeffrey's eyes and responded, "I do."

"Jeffrey, do you take Raven to be your wife for now and forever?"

"I do."

"Now, in front of all these witnesses and before your God, I pronounce that you are married for now and forever."

Jeffrey took Raven into his arms and kissed her long and hard. The crowd cheered. They threw flowers at the couple and sang an African wedding song as the couple turned and waved to them. The drums began to beat, and the flute played as the couple celebrated their marriage with their crew. Everyone gathered around to eat and drink with the newlyweds. The party continued until late into the night when Raven and Jeffrey finally retired to her cabin.

Raven slept until mid-morning. She awoke to Captain Billings ruffling through her hair. She realized something was missing once the morning haze had left her brain. Jeffrey had risen already and left Raven undisturbed.

Raven rose and stood before the wash pan as she bathed before dressing. She looked around the cabin and saw the jade gown spread out over the table where she had disrobed the night before. She collected the gown and hung it in the cabinet before donning her usual attire of leather britches, linen shirt, and leather waistcoat. She looked in the mirror and tossed her hair about to even out the curls.

A knock came at her door.

"Come in."

Jeffery entered the cabin carrying a tray of food and drink for them to share. Mr. Hardy had prepared eggs, salted pork, and various fruits for the new couple's first breakfast. As the newlywed couple sat at the table to enjoy their meal, Captain Billings joined them, sitting on the table. Raven peeled a banana and handed it to the monkey, who meticulously munched on the fruit.

Jeffrey asked, "What now?"

Raven replied, "Well, we could get back into bed."

Jeffrey almost choked before replying, "No... I mean... yes, but what I meant was... what are your plans for the crew? Will we sail? If so, where?"

"Well, I've been thinking. It's the right time of year to find some Spanish Galleons traveling through the Caribbean. They will be loaded with gold if they come from South America."

"Yes, that is intriguing. But what if they are traveling in large groups together? How will we attack with only the two ships?"

"We attack from behind. We'll take out the last ship in the convoy, then move to the next until our hulls are full."

"Sounds like a plan, my love."

Raven smiled at Jeffrey's comment with the added tag, "My love."

"That's Captain Love to you."

Once they finished breakfast, Raven said, "Shall we get started?"

They left the cabin together and met John and Attila on the quarter-deck. When Raven looked over the rail toward the *Sea Witch*, she found Alexander and Pharaoh were waiting for her instructions as they stood near the helm.

Raven called over to Pharaoh, asking, "Is everyone aboard?"

"Aye, Mrs. Hamilton!"

Raven glared at Pharaoh as he and Alexander smiled at Pharaoh's jest.

"Alright, you two. I'm still the Red Raven."

"Aye, Captain."

Raven asked John, "Are we ready?"

"Aye, Raven."

She spoke loud enough for everyone on both ships to hear her.

"We sail for the Caribbean. Set a course for Barbados. We'll sail to the southernmost tip and resupply. Then, we'll scan the seas for any ships coming from the west. If we get separated along the way, we'll meet at the place they call Silver Sands."

Everyone acknowledged her orders and commenced preparations to launch the ships. The *Sea Witch* and *Raven's Destiny* left the Robin's

Nest a little past noon. They sailed west for ten days, running parallel to the equator. Seven days later, they were still 1200 miles from Barbados.

Mtamu was posted in the crow's nest when she spotted a tiny vessel drifting to their north. She called down and said, "Raven, I see a small boat floating directly north of us. I can't tell if anyone is in the boat."

Raven took out her spyglass and searched the waters to the north, but couldn't spot anything from her vantage point.

Raven turned to Isaac Finch and ordered, "90º north, Mr. Finch."

"Aye, Raven."

Isaac turned the wheel a little at a time until the ship's compass pointed north. The *Sea Witch* followed *Destiny*, not knowing why she had turned so abruptly north. The ships fought against the winds, making only six knots as they sailed. Raven moved to the ship's bow, searching for the vessel Mtamu had seen.

An hour later, Mtamu called from the crow's nest again, "Raven! I can see someone lying at the bottom of the boat. But I can't tell if they are alone or if there is more than one."

Raven looked through her spyglass again and spotted the small boat bouncing in the waves, but she still couldn't see anyone in the tiny vessel.

Raven called back to John, "Launch one of the dories with ten men to retrieve that boat."

John waved his acknowledgment and sent Seremala and nine others out to bring the boat and whatever was in it back to *Destiny*.

They rowed out to meet the tiny boat and reached it within twenty minutes. As they reached the craft, they discovered it was like none other they had ever seen. The little boat wasn't made of wood; it was constructed of some material they had never seen before. Seremala reached out to grab the boat and discovered it was made of a pliable cloth-like material. Inside the boat were three men. Seremala reached over to check to see if any of them were alive. As he reached over, the first man stirred slightly. His lips were parched, and his skin was red and sunburned. He whispered something without opening his eyes, but Seremala couldn't understand what was said.

Seremala took a waterskin and poured a small amount into the man's mouth. The man coughed. As Seremala pulled the water away, the man reached for more.

"Easy, my friend. Don't drink too fast."

He allowed the stranger to take another sip before moving over to the other two in the boat. Seremala discovered all three men were still alive, but only just. After allowing each man to drink enough water to revive themselves, they were moved into the dory and rowed back to *Destiny*.

As they rowed back to the ship, the first man looked at Seremala and asked, "Where are we?"

"You are in the Atlantic Ocean, about 1200 miles from Barbados. What is your name?"

The man struggled as if trying to remember who he was. "I...I am.... Charles Taylor."

"Mr. Taylor, I am Seremala. Where is your ship?"

"Ship? Oh, no. We weren't on a ship. We were in an airplane."

Confused, Seremala repeated, "An airplane?"

"Yes, we were flying over Bermuda when a storm suddenly appeared and collided with us. It knocked out our instruments, and we lost control of the plane and had to bail out before crashing."

Seremala was again confused by the strange talk. "What is an airplane?

Now, Taylor was confused. "You've never heard of an airplane?"

"No."

"Well, I guess it's like a ship, but instead of sailing on the ocean, it flies in the air."

Seremala looked at the others in his crew and smiled. They all began to laugh uncontrollably.

Then Seremala asked Taylor, "Why did you have to bail out the ship if it was flying? How did water get into it?"

Taylor was now confused.

"Oh! No, we didn't bail the ship out. We bailed out of the ship. We jumped out of the ship before it crashed into the ocean."

Seremala nodded without saying another word to the stranger.

Taylor looked over at his men and asked, "George? Walter? Are you alright?"

"Yes, sir, Lieutenant."

Taylor said, "We were mighty lucky you men came along. We would have died out here without fresh water. Where are you taking us?"

Seremala pointed toward the two ships. Taylor glanced over, then looked harder. He couldn't believe his eyes. It looked like two square-rigged ships were floating in the middle of the ocean, a few thousand feet away.

"Are you men making a movie?"

Seremala replied, "What is a movie?"

Taylor decided he had best not ask any more questions. He might not like the answers he got. Instead, he and the others sat silently in the dory while Raven's crew rowed them closer to the ship.

Raven stood at the rail, watching through her spyglass as the dory rowed closer and closer. She moved the spyglass from one individual to the other. She had the strangest feeling she had seen these men before, but where?

Slowly, the dory returned to the ship. Seremala threw a line up to the crew aboard *Destiny* to secure the dory from floating away. Each man climbed a rope ladder to the ship's main deck with Seremala in the lead. He led the three strangers to Raven and introduced them to her.

The strangers saw the beautiful young woman standing before them in leather garb, wearing a sword on her belt, and suddenly became speechless.

"Captain, these men were in the little boat we saw floating in the sea."

Raven looked at them suspiciously and said, "My name is Raven Ashworth, but everyone calls me the Red Raven. Who are you?"

Jeffrey felt his stomach flip as Raven introduced herself as Raven Ashworth. They hadn't discussed her name change. *Was it just a slight faux pas on her part?*

Taylor replied, "I am Lieutenant Charles Taylor, and these are my men, George Devlin and Walter Parpart."

"Did you say, Charles Taylor?"

"Well, yes. I did."

Raven felt faint, "Oh no!"

Comments By The Author

Dreams are funny things. How often have you awakened from your sleep, unable to remember what you had just dreamed? Other times, your dreams were so vivid that you were convinced they really happened. Many dreams come about because of something on our minds before we go to bed. Maybe a concern or worry that keeps nagging at us. Other times, we dream of things that happened to us many years ago that we thought we had forgotten.

Many of my dreams are recurring. I have nightmares about working for the Postal Service. I know I'm supposed to be retired, but I still keep getting called into work. Then, when I get there, I never have the right equipment to do the job.

Sometimes, I dream about my days as a security officer in Memphis, and other times, I dream of being back in college. People I haven't seen or heard from in many years tend to pop into my dreams.

Then there are the dreams where I have superpowers, like being able to fly or run with the speed of lightning. Other times, my dreams put me in recurring situations, like having to walk through a yard full of poisonous snakes or losing all of my teeth. The worst is needing to go to the bathroom, and every time I think I'm alright, someone, usually a female, walks into the room and evades my privacy. Sorry, I just can't go with someone watching me.

Just remember, your dreams are your own, and no one can tell you that what you dream is absurd or unlikely to happen. Who knows, maybe your dream will someday turn into a best-selling novel.

MLC

Author Bio

Michael L. Clark is an award-winning historical fiction author. He and his wife of more than 40 years live in the Pensacola, Florida area after Clark retired from the U. S. Postal Service in 2022. His stories captivate readers with a wide range of subject matter, whether it be time-travel in the frontier of Tennessee, riding with the Pony Express in 1860, or sailing with pirates in the early 18th century. Clark's stories will leave you begging for more. Be sure to see all of his works on his website **www.author-michaellclark.com**

Other Titles By Michael L. Clark

The Shimmering Trilogy

The Shimmering
The Diary of Gus Childers
The Prophet

Young America Series

Ambush at Horse Creek

The Red Raven Pirate Series

The Red Raven
Raven's Destiny
Raven's Lost Island